LOOKING FOR

This book is a work of fiction. Names, characters, organisations, places, events and incidents are either products of the author's imagination or are used fictitiously.
All rights reserved.

C J Galtrey.

LOOKING FOR SHONA

A night of madness using a Ouija Board in January 2012 would change Liam Egan's life and the people he cared about forever.

The search to find the love of his life would take him to places he would never have imagined.

This story is about one man's struggle with the present day and the life he believes he led in the past and what it all mean's.

For my beautiful sister Linda for all the support and belief she has given me.

My first love story set in Ireland, London and the Caribbean.

C J Galtrey

LOOKING FOR SHONA

It was 3.30am when I woke, sweating and shaking what was happening to me? This had gone on for five weeks every night at the same time and exactly 3.30am I would wake every morning after these dreams. My name is Liam Egan; I am an ordinary guy with a good education, great friends and a well paid job.

My story is possibly hard to comprehend but I am writing this knowing that my time here is limited. It was the 12th January 2012 and I was celebrating my birthday with friends. Most of my friends are my work colleagues, we work hard and we play hard. The city traders or Yuppies as the Margaret Thatcher era labelled us.

The night this started, I was with Jamie Trench, a trader like myself and possibly my best mate. Millie Trench, wife of Jamie Trench, Jayne Tupton, a mate from University, Stan Woods, his real name is Thomas but for some reason we all called him Stan nobody could remember why though. Then there was Jenny Fenney my immediate boss from work. her partner Ian Ludlow, my rugby playing mate and Glofachs Lindley, a trader who worked with Jamie, although I do use the word trader loosely with regard to Glofachs. Glofachs seemed to invite himself to anyone's party. The joke at work was that Glofachs would turn up for the opening of a fridge door.

The reason I am telling you about all these people is that they were all there the night this dreadful nightmare began. My ancestors arrived in Liverpool in 1831, that is what my father had told me and his father had told him. My father was very proud of his Irish ancestry and would always remind me of this fact whenever Ireland played football or rugby, there was never any doubt who I was expected to support. My brother and I had been brought up in Liverpool, my dad worked on the building sites. Mum worked at The Cabbage Hall pub she cooked, cleaned and did bar work. So you can guess we were not rich. Mum and Dad tried to give me and Fergal my brother the best they

4

could but to be honest we were the poor kids on the council estate, a notorious estate called Mulgawn Estate, Liverpool 16.

Fergal my brother excelled at sport and I for some reason was considered clever. I secretly wanted to be my older brother. I loved rugby but never achieved the dizzy heights that my big brother did, who played twice for Ireland. I meanwhile played lower league. I digress. Let me take you back to the 12th of January. We had drunk copious amount of champagne and Jaeger bombs. Jayne asked us all to go back to her apartment in Canary Wharf. This was quite a common thing on somebody's birthday. We all staggered back to Jayne's and she ordered a Chinese to be delivered.

More drink and the Chinese food followed, but the next thing to happen was the thing that changed my life forever. Glofachs suggested a Ouija board game would be fun. The board was set up and we all sat round Jayne's dining table. The letters were placed round in a circle, with another two card's with the words 'Yes' and 'No' printed on them. We were told to concentrate and clear our minds. I thought clearing our minds would not be difficult with the amount of drink we had drunk; it certainly had dulled all our senses.

Glofachs asked the question "Does anybody want to speak to me?" Nothing happened. He asked again and still nothing happened. It was my turn I gave my name "Liam Egan does anybody want to speak to me"?

Immediately the glass started to move to the "Yes" card. I looked at Glofachs. "Ask who it is Liam?" "Who are you?" I asked, the glass moved to the letter C then A then B then H then it stopped. I glanced at Glofachs as it started again, really quickly, it went to the letter A and it finished with the letter N. I said "Cabhan, is that your name?" The glass moved quickly to the Yes card. "What is your surname?" Nothing happened. I tried further questions but nothing seemed to get the glass going. Everybody had a turn around the table but nothing else came up. Just as we were about to give up, I turned to Glofachs and said "You were pushing that glass Glofachs, who has a name like Cabhan?"

Suddenly the glass flew off the table and smashed against the sideboard, shattering glass everywhere. "You know what? This is silly, let's call it a night" "I agree Jayne". We all thanked her and left. I shared a taxi with Glofachs and as I got out at my apartment Glofachs said, "Be careful, that was real tonight" "I know you were clowning about". "Liam I wasn't" said Glofachs. I didn't feel concerned because I was pretty sure this was a wind up, but that night the dreams or rather life changing nightmares began.

That night I fell into a deep sleep.

The first thing I remember was the heat. It was so hot and the vision of the man I saw had on a ripped shirt and a pair of khaki coloured trousers that were rolled up to just below the knees. He had no shoes on and with him were probably twenty men and this big guy with a bull whip. He took

7

great delight in whipping anybody that spoke or was perceived not to be working hard enough. All the men in the line were Negroes, but they spoke English, there was just one who was white and his name was Cabhan.

Not too much happened that first night, I woke sweating as if I had been on the line working and my back felt sore, although there was nothing showing on my back when I checked. Later that day whilst at work, I started to remember other things. The date this started for me was 1627. I was living in Ireland on the West Coast, right on the shore line at Claw Bay. My father had been killed fighting the Spanish in the Anglo –Spanish War a couple of years earlier. I was fourteen. I remember the day the Moorish pirates raided our homes in our little village. Most of the men folk had been killed fighting at Cadiz. One of the pirates, I remembered, knocked me to the floor and hit my mum and sister this stuck in my memory for many years. I was taken away, as were two other boys of my age. The rest of the village was ransacked and burnt.

LOOKING FOR SHONA

We had no idea where they were taking us, I heard somebody say we would be indentured servants. I had not got a clue what that meant. The journey was long, the two boys from my village fell sick, and when the first one died we were laid in a huddle trying to keep warm. One of the pirates picked him up and we heard them say throw him to the sharks. The other boy Dermot protested so they threw him over as well, he was so weak but he tried to save his friend. This was something else that would haunt me, because I just sat by and watched. We landed on an island, after what seemed like an age at sea, we were lined up and told to open our mouths while they checked our teeth. We were stripped and I remember bending down and one of the pirates whipping me with his bull whip.

Feeling quite ill after such an awful night's sleep I headed off for work. My desk was next to Jamie Trench's we were best mates. Next to Jamie was Glofachs, he was a bit of a prat and not very good at his job. We would be going at it, trading full bore and he would be talking about what we were doing that night etc.

This is going to sound silly but my back actually felt sore and my dream was very vivid. It was so sore that I had to ask Jamie to come to the toilet with me and check if he could see anything. Of course he couldn't and he asked me why. I was just about to tell him what had happened when bloody Glofach came in. "Wondered where you two were, you're not an item are you?" and he laughed. "Oh shut up you prick" I shouted at him as I was leaving. I heard him ask Jamie what he had done. Jamie being the mate he was just said that I was a bit under the cosh with some of the trading.

That night we managed to shake off Glofachs and decided to have a meal, just me and Jamie, so I could off load my problem. Jamie liked Italian food so he chose Sapori D' Italia which roughly translated means tastes of Italy. This was his favourite restaurant. I think he quite fancied the thought that he was of Italian descent, with his slicked back black hair and dark eyes. I remember thinking I wish I had been Italian I wouldn't be having this crap now!!

The restaurant was very plush with statues everywhere, the type you see in Rome. All the waiters were Italian, with crisp white shirts and black aprons folded and worn round their waist.

We were shown to our table by a waiter and shown the wine list. As I say Jamie thought of himself as Italian, so he ordered the most expensive wine and ordered it in Italian which made the waiter smile. He was probably thinking, "What a pair of prat's"

The wine arrived with Jamie doing his wine connoisseur bit, smelling the cork, then the wine and all that rubbish. We had chosen our meals; I went for the "Tris di Crostini" followed by "Gamberoni alla Diavola". I love King Prawns so I was made up that they were on the menu. Jamie chose "Alla Livornese" followed by "Fegato alla Veneziana". "I love liver Liam, and the way they do the calves liver

11

is the best". "Bloody hate liver of any kind mate". "You're a bloody peasant Liam". I was thinking wait until I tell him about my dreams, he's probably right!!!

"So come on then, what's troubling you mate? Not got one of your harems up the duff have you?" "What bloody harem? I've forgotten the last time I took somebody out". "If it's not that, then you are about to tell me you are coming out of the closet? And that's what the episode with your back in the toilet was all about" and he laughed. "So Glofachs was right?" "Don't be daft. I need to tell somebody about the weird things happening since we played on that Ouija board". Just then the starters arrived. "Well at least you haven't lost your appetite mate, even if you are losing your marbles".

Liam was more interested in telling Jamie his story about Cabhan than eating his starter, although Jamie was soon tucking into his. "That night at Jayne's flat, I thought Glofachs was pushing the glass and you were all probably in on it, with it being my birthday, but when I got home I was thinking what a prat Glofachs was to think I am that daft to be taken in by you all pushing a glass round a board. With the drink we had consumed I fell into a deep sleep and that's when this started". The waiter took their starter plates away. "Is there something wrong Sir?" Liam had hardly touched his starter. "No, sorry it was very nice". The waiter looked puzzled, but went away. "So what happened then Liam, or is it Cabhan?" "Don't take the piss Jamie, I am seriously worried" "Sorry mate, only trying to make light of it, so what happened?" "I dreamt I lived in Claw Bay, on the West Coast of Ireland, it was 1625 and we had heard that pirates were ransacking coastal villages and taking all the able bodied men and children that looked strong and were then killing the others and burning the villages".

"We thought we were quite safe. Most of the men folk had not returned from fighting in Cadiz, although in our family I was head of the household because father had been killed in the fighting. We weren't a big village and we thought the

13

shallow rock waters in the bay would stop any ships coming in as there were larger villages with better access than ours" "So why did they come then?" "I don't know why, or how, but they did. They took me and two other boys. We were fourteen years old. To cut a long story short, one of the boys became ill and they said he would be no good where we were going, so they threw him to the sharks. The other boy protested, so they did the same to him. I remember in the dream thinking I was a coward because I just watched" "Liam it's a bloody dream don't worry about it".

The waiter appeared with the main course, again Liam was busy telling Jamie his story that he hardly ate a thing. When the waiter cleared the table he looked at Liam strangely, but it went over Liam's head, he needed to try and get Jamie to understand.

"Go on then what happened next?" "I remember feeling sick every day and the brutal pirates who would whip you if you got out of line. We landed on an island where we were clearly expected, I think it was Barbados. The only reason I say that is, I looked at some images after the dream and I felt very uncomfortable, I may be wrong".

"So you are on this island, what happened next?" "I just remember being lashed with a bull whip and the excruciating pain that was inflicted on somebody so young. After that nothing, until I woke up and my back was sore, as if I had really been whipped".

"Look mate, it's a good story and I am sure you believe in what you say, but it was just a dream. You had loads of booze, we played a stupid game and it spooked you, that's it. So are we having a sweet or going clubbing?" "I don't want any more food", "You have lost your appetite mate, let me pay the bill and we can go to Sticky Tina's for an hour it's Motown night. You never know you might pick up a dusky maiden" and Jamie laughed.

Liam felt he had to go with Jamie but he wasn't really bothered. Once inside Sticky Tina's, Jamie was soon on the dance floor with his Ray Ban's on. Liam did think he looked Italian to be fair. Liam got the drinks and sat down on a curved leather seat, watching his mate make a prat of himself. After a few minutes a black girl asked if she could join him. "Yes of course", Liam gestured for her to sit down. "Hi, my name is Joan". Liam got up from the seat and thrust his hand forward to shake Joan's hand. Joan was tall almost six feet, Liam thought, and with her high heels on she looked about six foot four. She wore a white dress, with contrasting black shoes; she looked remarkably like Halle Berry with her hair cut short. "What do you do for a living Liam" she asked. "I'm a trader in the city. What about you?" "I work for the Red Cross, so I travel a fair bit". "That must be so interesting Joan?" "Yes, I love it. Do you mind if I ask, are your family Irish?" "What makes you think that?" "Just your name, I hope you don't think I was being nosey?" said Joan.

"No, not at all, my roots are in Ireland on the West Coast, but my family came to Liverpool in 1831 looking for work". "What about you?" "My family are from Barbados, not sure how we got here, but I would think for the same reason, looking for work. I grew up in London". "Wow, what a coincidence" said Liam. "What is?" "Oh nothing, just something I am reading about at the moment".

Just then Jamie came for his drink. "Not taken you long Liam to find a pretty maiden. We call him Rock Socks at work, but I can't tell you why though. I'm Jamie pleased to meet you". "Likewise I'm Joan". "Are you two coming for a dance?" Joan looked at Liam in a shy way. "Would you like to Joan?" "Come on then, let's see Rock Socks shake his booty" and she laughed. Liam looked at this beautiful woman moving onto the dance floor. They never went back to the table, but danced until 2.00 am, when the DJ finally put the main lights up and thanked everyone for coming. "I'll get our coats Liam" "Thanks Jamie".

Liam felt nervous to ask Joan for a date she was such a beauty he could imagine every guy in the place would like to ask her out. He threw caution to the wind as his grandma used to say "Faint heart never won fair lady". They both stared at each other. Liam started to ask Joan and she started the conversation at the same time. "Sorry no after you Joan" he said. "Well I hope you don't think I am being too forward but could we meet up again? I have had a lovely night Liam" "Yes I would love to". And at that they exchanged mobile numbers. Joan's friend shouted that their taxi was waiting, she pecked Liam on the cheek and left, leaving Liam feeling he was floating on air.

"Come on lover boy". "Sorry Jamie I was miles away" said Liam. "Who wouldn't be with bloody Halle Berry you lucky git. Are you seeing her again?" "Well I have got her number that is if she answers at all after you told her my nickname, you dick". "She needs to know who she is dealing with old lad" and Jamie laughed and they got in the taxi. "Why don't you bring her over to ours Saturday night and me and Millie will cook a meal?" "I don't know mate, good of you to offer, but will she think I am rushing things?" "Don't be daft. She might feel there is safety in numbers, especially with your nick name". "Ok I will let you know as long as you are sure Millie won't mind". "Flippin heck, you know Millie, she loves entertaining and showing off her culinary skills". "Ok thanks mate I will call Joan tomorrow".

The following day on the trading floor, Jenny Fenney had Glofachs into the office and told him his trading figures weren't good enough and that he had to get his act in gear. While Glofachs was getting his bollocking, Jamie asked Liam about the dreams and did he have another one last night? "Funnily enough, no I didn't Jamie, I fell straight to sleep and slept well" "Told you it was a one off, it was the booze and that stupid bloody game, forget about it now mate" "Yeah you're right

Jamie, thanks for being a good mate". "Have you phoned Miss Berry yet?" "No I haven't and her name is Joan. I'll call her at lunchtime". Glofachs came out of his meeting with Jenny and was gutted. "Never seen you so quiet Glofachs". "She just gave me my last warning; my parents will go mental if I lose this job". "Then knuckle down". "You are right Liam" said a despondent Glofachs.

The lunchtime bell went. "Are we going to Diamond Lil's for Oysters lads?" "Glofachs, you would be better grabbing a sandwich at your desk and showing Jenny you are committed, don't you think?" "Guess so, well have one for me lads". Jamie and Liam left but decided to just have a sandwich at Starbucks. Jamie ordered and Liam phoned Joan. "Hi Joan its Liam Egan" "Hello Liam, thank you for last night, I really enjoyed it" "I wondered if you fancied coming with me to Jamie's, you met him last night, his wife Millie, has invited us over for a meal" "Jamie is married?" she asked. "Yes why?" "Well nothing really, just that he was in the club until 2am this morning". "Oh Jamie loves dancing. He would never do anything untoward, he absolutely adores Millie, but Millie is a teacher and she doesn't like being out late on a school day. It works for them Joan".

"Sorry, I wasn't being judgemental". "Sure you weren't, probably does seem a bit weird but I have known Liam and Millie for ever and it's never been anything different. Please say you will come, I would love you to meet Millie". "Liam, I would love to". "Ok, text me your address" said Jamie. "Don't worry, send me Jamie and Millie's address and I will get a taxi straight there". "Ok whatever is best for you. If you could be there for 7.30pm on Saturday night that would be great". "Looking forward to it already Liam. Look I have to go, I am at a conference and they are calling us back into the conference room". "Ok see you Saturday". "Look forward to it". And the call ended.

Jamie came back with two Bacon and Brie Toasties and two Americano coffees. "Ok mate, we are on for Saturday" said Liam.

"Brilliant we will have a good night mate. Not seen you like this in a long time". "Well you know I have been out with quite a few girls, but somehow this one seems special". "She is a looker mate and what a figure". "Do you know Jamie it's not even that? There is just something about her".

"What about poor old Glofachs?" "It's his own bloody fault, he is forever clowning around and he missed that big deal with GLS Rubber didn't he? I know that didn't go down too well with Jenny". "I know but he doesn't mean any harm, it's his upbringing. Moved from one public school to another, pressure from his parents to be educated it's all wrong". "Suppose you are right, I would not have swapped where I was brought up; at least it taught me life skills".

Liam and Jamie headed back to work, the afternoon was soon over and Liam headed back to his flat. He spent the evening reading. Liam enjoyed reading, mainly history or sometimes a biography. His mind wandered to his meeting with Joan he didn't know her surname and had only met her once, but knew he was falling for her in a big way.

Liam climbed into bed and was soon fast asleep his job wasn't physical but mentally it was quite shattering.

You may now be wondering where this is all going, this was the second time I had the dream. I woke exactly at 3.30am again. I was sweating. I felt hot this time and thirsty, very thirsty, then I started remembering the things that had happened while I was asleep.

I was stood naked in a line, all the other men were black, and there were white men with bull whips. After the last whipping, I knew to stand bolt upright and never have eye contact with them. They stood us on wooden boxes and there were five or six very well dressed men. I remember thinking I wanted to be back in Claw Bay. I felt scared and frightened. I was shaking with fear. A man with a wooden hammer started barking out numbers I didn't understand. When the wooden hammer fell, they took the first in line away. We were all shackled together and the iron rings rubbed into my skin. It was my turn next, four or five of these well-dressed men, checked me over they seemed obsessed with my teeth. The man with the wooden hammer said "The only white boy here today, you can breed from this one gents".

They started shouting numbers out and eventually the man with the hammer slammed it down hard and said "Sold to Humphrey Slaley Morton". The man was quite elderly with quite long grey hair. As he paid, he looked at me, but told another man to put me on a cart.

Now I was awake, I felt this is getting out of hand, but what do I do? I wish I had never played that stupid game. Who is Cabhan? Was he an ancestor or just a troubled spirit that we had disturbed on that fateful night?

Nothing more happened for the rest of the week which I was pleased about and maybe that was it. I had tonight to look forward to, the meal at Jamie and Millie's with the beautiful Joan. I arrived at their house at 7.15pm, Millie met me at the door and I gave her some flowers and a bottle of champagne. Jamie had a lovely house, beautiful wife and was a really nice man. He had been a good mate to me and had taught me a lot at work he really deserved everything he had.

"Scotch mate?" "Why not Jamie" "You ok?" "Bit nervous mate, I really like this one". Bang on 7.30pm the doorbell rang, Millie went to answer it. "Come in Joan, so nice to meet you". "She's here mate, Millie just let her in". Liam got up and trying to be cool, spilt his whisky. "I am so sorry Millie". "Don't worry about it, the carpet will clean" Joan looked stunning, she had on an orange dress, cut just above her knees with a cropped cardigan in blue, with blue shoes and a matching blue clutch handbag. Liam gave her a peck on the cheek.

This was Millie's type of night she loved cooking and entertaining. She poured everyone a glass of champagne and placed the first course on the table. "I hope you like sea food Joan". "Love sea food Millie" she replied. "Well these are Seared Scallops with a cauliflower salad and a Lemon Butter emulsion". "This is gorgeous Millie". They began their starters and Millie started the cross examination of my beautiful Joan.

"If you don't mind me saying, Joan is like Millie, quite an old fashioned name? It's so lovely and really suits you". "It was my Grandma's name and I believe her mother was also Millie". "Where do you work Millie?" "Knightsbridge Public School" replied Millie. "Guessing it's a bit elite then". "Yes suppose you could say that. What about you?". Joan replied, "I work for the British Red Cross as Director of Overseas Development" "Really, that must be amazing" "Yes, I love it. I travel a lot I see a lot of horrific things but if I only help one person a day then I feel I am doing my bit".

The boys were busy talking about the upcoming England versus Ireland football game, obviously, Jamie standing his corner on England and Liam for Ireland. Liam thought how much he was enjoying the night; the dreadful dreams were a distant memory being around such nice people. "Ok you two, be quiet for the main course. Lobster Thermidor which is Blue Crab with a white wine and Dijon Mustard sauce everyone enjoy". "Millie this is fabulous". "Thank you Liam, that's worth all the effort".

"So how did you two meet then?" "I was out with some old school friends at Sticky Tina's and I saw Liam sat alone. My friends had gone dancing, so I plucked up courage and went over and had a chat". "Lucky man Liam" "You bet Millie". "I suppose my daft as a brush husband was dancing like a loon on the dance floor? He really does think he is John Travolta don't you sweetie?" "No I think John Travolta thinks he is me" "You are so funny Jamie" and Joan laughed showing the smile of a Hollywood actress. "Has anyone ever told you that you look like Halle Berry Joan?" "If I wasn't black you would see me blushing. I have been asked a few times. One lady was so persistent that I must sign her tee shirt, that I did just to get her off my back" "Forger hey?" "Don't Liam I feel bad about it to this day".

"Ok who has got room for a dessert? The boys obviously do what about you Joan?" "Just a small piece, what is it you have made?" "It's my speciality, I always make it for Liam it's called Carrageen Citrus Pudding" "It sounds lovely and refreshing but only a small piece, I have to watch my figure" "As if!! You have a wonderful figure do you go to the gym?" "No Millie, I am lucky I think it's a gene thing" "Well you are lucky Joan".

"The taste of Orange and Lemons is great, but what is that underlying taste?" "It's seaweed!!" "Really? Wow it really is good". The evening was rounded off with coffee and Millie's homemade chocolates. "I arranged for my taxi for 11.30pm and he just texted to say he is downstairs". "Ok I will walk you down" "Are you staying in the spare room Liam?" "If you two don't mind" "Of course not mate" "Lovely to see you again Joan" "Thank you for a lovely night Jamie. Thank you

Millie I have had a lovely evening"
"Anytime Joan, I'm sure we will be seeing
more of you". Liam and Joan went down
stairs before they got to the taxi they
kissed passionately. "Can I see you again
Joan?" "I have a wedding evening party
next Saturday; do you want to come
along?" "I would love to". "Ok, I will call
you in the week. I fly out to Nigeria for
three days next week and I'm not back
until Friday morning".

Liam climbed the stairs back to Millie and
Jamie's apartment. He could have flown
up he felt so elated. How did he manage to
catch this one? She was stunning. Jamie
had poured himself, Liam and Millie a
nightcap of Brandy and Baileys. "Liam
she is a lovely girl" "Thanks Millie, I have
weird feeling for her" "Too much
information old lad" "No not like that
sewer mind, I mean she seems special to
me already, I have never had that with a
girl before".

"Possibly found the one Liam" "Do you
think so Millie?" "Well I think what you
are describing is love" "Blimey, never

thought I would ever find true love"
"Good luck to you mate" They finished
their drinks and made their way to bed.

Liam was soon fast asleep, but yet again
he woke with a start. He looked across at
the bedside alarm clock, it showed
3.30am. What the hell was the
significance of that? He sat up in bed and
started remembering his dream again.

The cart he was put out on by Humphrey
Slaley Morton's overseer had two black
men, himself and a scruffy looking dog,
that was scratching itself all the time as if
it had fleas. The black men never looked
up they were all shackled together but
there was no conversation. Cabhan wasn't
sure if they could speak English anyway.
They eventually arrived at a sugar
plantation, although Cabhan didn't know
what it was at the time. They were taken
down a dirt track, past a grand white
house with a porch all the way round it.
He could see white women on the porch
eating and drinking, they were all in their
finery, beautiful long dresses of all
colours. They were taken down to a

wooden hut. There were black people everywhere, men, women and children. The children seemed happy enough. I spotted one white face, a man, he was older than me I would say he was about twenty eight. The overseer got us down off the cart and undid our shackles then he lined us up with bull whip in hand.

"Let me tell you the rules. When you are working in the fields cutting the sugar cane you will be shackled. When you are by the house, you won't be. If you decide to run away we will find you. You will then be severely whipped and then we will hang you from the nearest tree as a lesson to anyone else. While I have been overseer we have only had five of your type run away. All five were caught beaten then hung, so remember my words. The overseer looked at Cabhan "What's your name?" "Cabhan" I said quietly. "I am Mr Grapes, remember my name boy and when I speak to you look at the floor, do not look at me then we won't have a problem".

He turned to the other two, "What are your names?" For the first time the biggest black man spoke, he was giant of a man, all of six foot five with massive muscular arms. "My name is Jankay". The overseer, who was also a big man, squared up to Jankay. "So are you going to be a good boy or will I have to whip your nigger arse into shape?" "You will have no problem with me Sir" said Jankay, "Good, glad to hear it". I had never heard the word nigger before, in fact I had never seen a black man until I was taken from Claw Bay. Mr Grapes turned to the other black man. "What's your name?" The man tried to speak, then Jankay spoke for him. "Oday Sir, his name is Oday". Grapes got angry, "I wasn't talking to you" "Sir he has no tongue, they cut it out so he can't speak". "Well let me tell you Black Boy, you speak when I tell you too or I will cut out your tongue clear?" "Yes Sir". I wasn't to know at the time but Oday and Jankay would become very much needed friends.

That was all I could remember and I fell back to sleep. Millie woke me up. "Bacon sandwich Liam?" "Great thanks Millie".

Liam quickly showered then sat down at the breakfast table. "Blimey did you have a nightmare last night?" "I don't know why?" "You woke me and Millie up, we could hear you talking to somebody, a Mr Grapes?" "I am so sorry, this is really embarrassing" "Why?" "I had another dream again" "What dream and what do you mean again?" asked Millie "Have you not told Millie, Jamie?" "Told me what?" Jamie answered, "Liam keeps having nasty dreams, ever since the Ouija board thing the other week" "Have you seen anybody about it Liam?" "No, not into doctors" "I wasn't thinking of a doctor, I was thinking more like a regression specialist" "What would that do?" "Well, I read in one of my magazines about a woman that had dreams, like you are having for almost five years, then eventually she went to one of these regression people and apparently they take you back in time and she spilled the whole story out and has never had a dream again". "I don't know Millie, I am not into that sort of thing". "What harm can it do if it helps you?" "I'll see" "Well I will keep the magazine because it has the regression specialists' address in it and you might change your mind"

"Listen, thanks very much for a great evening yet again, and I am so sorry if I kept you two up" "Hey anytime Liam, just don't get depressed with those dreams. I am sure that woman in the magazine would sort you". Liam gave Millie a peck on the cheek and shaking Jamie's hand he set off for home.

He walked alongside the Thames and through a couple of old streets towards his flat in a renovated warehouse. Liam had lived at the warehouse for almost three years. It was a nice area, there was never any trouble. Most of the residents were professional people, about fifty percent only used their flats all the time choosing to go home at the weekends. So the exercise room and the indoor heated pool were quite at the weekends which suited Liam.

He opened his flat door everything was very modern, colour co-ordinated electrical goods. His kitchen was cream with black marble worktops. The flat had two bedrooms both en-suite. When Liam bought it, he found the repayments very hard but as he became better at his job he had paid large amounts off and was hoping to be mortgage free by 2017. Liam sat down to watch the golf. Could Spieth beat McIlroy in the Masters play off. Golf was another passion of Liam's.

It was 2.00am in the morning when the game was over so Liam climbed into bed. The dreams started almost immediately. Was this ever going to end? Cabhan was shown where he would be living with Jankay and Oday. He was given some fatty meat and a small piece of cornbread, the black woman that gave it me seemed nice. Jankay said the slave owners didn't feed you, so the women would cook what they could for the men folk. That is also when I got my first shock, he told me that all the black women would like me because if they had children by me the children would have a better life, because the fairer your skin quite often meant you were given work at the big house or sometimes given an apprenticeship. If you were totally black then your life would be spent in the fields doing hard labour and they didn't want that for their children.

"How old are you white boy?" "I am fourteen Mister", I said. Jankay and Oday laughed. "You calling a nigger Sir?", and they laughed again. I didn't understand but I would do in time. The food was just bearable but I missed my mums cooking. Jankay told me that I would probably be in gang two, with being so young and besides the work wasn't as hard in gang two. The hard work was done by the black men and women in gang one. He told me never to answer back to the Boss man or he would whip me, always agree and always call him Sir. He told me I had to work hard and eventually, because of my skin colour, I might get an apprenticeship or at least a job in the big house. Oday just sat and listened. "How did Oday lose his tongue Jankay?" "We were both brought here from our home land, it happened at the last place we were made to work at, before being sold to come here. Oday got into a fight with the Overseer, he made a mess of him so they beat him real bad and then when he was almost dead, they cut out his tongue so that he could never answer back again".

"Get some sleep boy, you are going to need it tomorrow". I lay down on some straw they had provided, the lady that had brought the food also gave me three pairs of underpants and a pair of shoes they were to last me a whole year!! I found it hard to sleep, I could hear the rats squirreling around in the bedding and big Jankay snored like my granddad Seamus used to when he lived with us in Claw Bay.

I lay in this pit of despair wondering how this could be. My father had fought for the English in Cadiz and now he was dead and I was a slave in a foreign land what sort of King was he that would let this happen to his subjects? That was all I could remember about the dream but it felt so real.

LOOKING FOR SHONA

I got up it was almost 11.00am so I put my running gear on and ran five miles. I felt better once I was back the fresh air had cleared my mind a bit, it was then that I thought about what Millie had said. Should I go and see one of these Regression people or would that do more harm than good?

I realised this was starting to take over my life and the next day at work Jenny Fenney called me into the office. "Are you ok Liam?" "Why Jenny?" "Well to be honest your performance figures are way down to normal and I have watched you and you seem in a dream. You do know this door is always open and what you tell me won't go any further" "I am fine thanks Jenny, been feeling a bit under the weather". How could I tell my boss about my messed up head? She would think I was a loon. I hadn't even told Joan. She seemed ok with my excuse and asked me if I was going bowling with everyone on Wednesday night. "I guess so" "Well not trying to match make but my friend from University is coming to stay for a week;

she is a Geordie lass, very pretty. She split from her husband about three months ago so I told her to come down to me for a week. You will like her Liam". I couldn't tell Jenny I was seeing somebody, not after I had just been let off with my figures so poor. I just acted daft. "Ok great, look forward to meeting her. Look Jenny I best get back and get some work done". "Ok Liam, will see you Wednesday then" "Look forward to it Jenny".

Liam realised he had to settle down and get his trading back on song so he hardly spoke for the next two days and luckily he had no dreams which certainly helped.

It was a cold February morning, how the seasons seem to have changed Liam thought. When he was a boy in Liverpool February always seemed to be raining and now it was heavy frosts in a morning.

Liam arrived at his work station ready for the day's action. "Have you heard about

Glofachs?" "No only just got here Jamie" "He was mugged last night and is on life support machine" "Really?" "Yeah he had been to a mate's house in Covent Garden and was coming back on the tube when two guys set about him. Apparently it was random attack they stole his phone and wallet and left him in a heap. Apparently there was a young girl in the corner but they didn't touch her" "Oh blimey, can he have visitors?" "Only family at the moment Liam, it's not very good apparently" "Poor old Glofachs he was harmless enough. Bet Jenny feels a bit bad about bollocking him the other day". "I know what you mean Jamie, but that's her job. Are you and Millie going bowling tonight?" "Yeah it's at Bowling World in Leicester Square. The bell sounded and they started trading. They both had a good day and it was soon home time. "Look mate will see you tonight at the bowling. Is Joan coming?" "No mate she is away until Friday and I'm missing her already" "Bloody hell Egan you're in love" "I think I am Jamie, I have never felt like this before, she has a strange hold on me.

Liam showered and dressed quite pleased with his day he put his comfortable light blue shirt on, the one he always used for bowling and a black pair of Chino's. He was just heading out when his phone rang. "Liam?" "Hey Joan how are you? How's the trip going?" "Good thanks how are you? Hope you are sat watching TV and not out on the pull" and she laughed. "Just going bowling actually, my boss organises these do's every now and again and it's sort of obligatory to go" "Yeah any excuse Mr Egan" "Joan this is going to sound really daft but I don't know your surname?" "Forde" "Oh ok Joan Ford" "No Liam, its Forde, with an e on the end of it" "That's unusual" "Apparently it is an Anglo Saxon name which is common in the US. Barbados, England and Ireland" "You might have some of that Irish blood in you" and Liam laughed.

"Listen Liam, I have to get back to the conference, I just thought I would see if we were going out on Friday night?" "Do you fancy a nice meal down the West End?" "Yeah that would be lovely, not bothered about clubbing, I will be too shattered after the flights" "Suit's me Joan, where shall I pick you up from?" "I will get a taxi to your place see you Friday about 7.30pm" and the phone went dead. Why doesn't she want me to know where she lives he thought?

Liam was the last to arrive, he was put in Jenny and Millie's team, both very competitive ladies, along with Ian, Jenny's boyfriend. The other team was Jamie, Jayne Tupton, Stan and Jenny's friend, the Geordie lass, Michelle Beevans. Michelle seemed like a nice girl, long flowing dark hair, very petite and very well dressed she oozed class Liam thought. But then Liam's only thoughts were for the lovely Joan. The two hours they spent bowling was a roaring success, as were all the nights Jenny put on, and of course her team won being the most competitive. "Does anyone fancy finishing off at a Casino?" I wasn't bothered but everyone said yes so I had little choice or it would have been frowned upon. They headed off to Lucky Jacks Casino dress code was quite relaxed here which he was surmising was the reason Jenny chose it with Liam being somewhat underdressed!!

Jamie, Liam and Ian headed straight for the Black Jack tables. They were buying ten pound chips, which were quite reserved for them seeing that they had such a good day on the floor. Liam put four chips on the first go, Jamie followed suit but Liam stuck ten chips down. Liam's first card was a three, Jamie's a Jack and Ian's a Queen. The dealer had a five of hearts a good card for the gambling three, as they called themselves. Both Jamie and Ian got aces next, with poor old Liam crashing out the bank also crashed, so a nice start for Jamie and Ian. The night carried on in the same vain, Ian was about fifteen hundred pounds up when they left, with Jamie eight hundred pounds up and poor Liam four hundred down. I knew I should have gone home when they asked me about going with them, he thought. It was now back to Jenny's for a take away.

They all sat eating their Chinese, when Jenny brought up the subject of the Ouija board game that they had played at

Jayne's place and how Liam had been the one that got the attention. Everyone was laughing. Liam could feel Jamie's eyes on him. Only he knew the trauma it had caused Liam. Ian said "Why don't we have another go at the Ouija board" They all agreed. I said I would love to play but I was not feeling to well, so I was going to make my way back home. I could see Jenny was disappointed, probably more for her friend Michelle, but I just could not go through that again.

By the time I had walked from Jenny's apartment to mine, it was almost 12.40am, so I dived straight into bed and was soon in a deep sleep. The dreams started almost immediately.

I was in a cart with thirteen other men and women. Mr Grapes was sat next to the driver. Grapes was an evil man. I later learned to hate his name, something forever embellished on my memory. The cart stopped next to the tall sugar cane field and we were split up. Oday and Jankay went into what they called number team one, I assumed that was the hardest team from what Jankay had told me last night. Five others followed them, they were all manacled by the legs. It was now that I met the man I would learn to hate, his name was James Coy or White Nigger Coy as they slaves called him behind his back. This man was a mountain of a man and one of the Slave Drivers. These jobs were given to some of the most powerful black slaves to keep the rest of us in check.

I was told that he took his name from his former owner, who had been a kindly gentleman very rare in Barbados; the owners were usually very nasty men. It certainly had not helped him, he was evil he delighted in abusing the women folk or whipping the men.

This was my first day and after an hour of cutting sugar cane, my hands were bleeding and sore. Coy grabbed me and asked me why I kept stopping. I didn't look at him I remembered what Jankay had told me. I said, "My hands are sore Sir" "So little Bog Arab your hands are sore are they?" "Yes Sir" "I can sort that for you, lean over the sugar cane pile". I was so frightened. "Now let me take your new shoes off". He then whipped me on the underside of my feet, my feet were pouring blood. One of the black slaves tried to help and he was mercifully beaten. Coy then said if I ever stop working again he would kill me. I was crying but nobody dare help and Cinti the slave who tried to help, was left in a poor way.

It was going dark when they told us to get back on the cart, they tied poor Cinti to the back and dragged him back with us. They said he hadn't worked, so he wasn't entitled to a lift. I wasn't sure how long I could stick this. When Jankay saw me, he wrapped my feet in sugar cane leaves, and then asked me what happened to Cinti. I told him what had happened. "How is Cinti have you seen him Jankay?" "Yes, he is swinging from the tree about ten yards up the track". The next thing I knew, I was awake shivering and the ball's of my feet were so sore I could hardly put them on the bedroom carpet it was 3.30am again. I got a mirror and looked at my feet they were a little red but nothing else, yet for a further ten minutes the pain was excruciating. Once the pain had subsided I fell back to sleep and woke to the sound of my phone ringing on my bedside table. It was still dark outside. "Hello" "Liam hurry up and open the door I am freezing down here". What had happened? Had I lost a day? Was it Friday now? I went downstairs opened the door and Joan looked at me as if I was an alien. "What are you doing in your pyjamas at this time of night?" I didn't know what to say. "Sorry I was just about to shower" "Where are we going to eat Liam?" "I am so sorry I haven't booked yet" "Its Friday night everywhere will be rammed".

They looked at each other, laughed and then fell into each other's arms in a passionate embrace. The bedroom was the only place this was going to end up. They were soon both naked, making passionate love. It felt like love to Liam, not just a sexual encounter, but the kind of love that people talked about and Liam had never encountered. Joan's skin was so smooth and perfect. Their love making came to fullness and they lay in each other arms, both breathless and hardly able to speak.

Liam played with Joan's short, dark hair, she was so beautiful. Suddenly Joan jumped up just as Liam touched her on the back of her shoulder blade. As she sat up Liam could see a nasty scar. "Oh I am sorry Joan, did I hurt you?" "It's just very tender; I apparently had it when I was born. My grandma said it was 'the mark' whatever that meant, but she told my Mum it meant I was here to stay". "If it hurts you, don't you think you should have it checked out?" "No, I have lived with it this long and it only hurts if I catch it. Are you hungry Liam?" "Starving, if I am honest". "Let's do something daft, let's go and get fish and chips and walk in the rain eating them" "I'm up for that". They dressed quickly, put their coats on and walked half a mile to a chippy. "Fish, chips and mushy peas, twice please" The old guy serving was a character and was telling jokes in his cockney accent. They left the chippy laughing as they ate their meal.

It was a beautiful night and I was feeling blessed to have met a lovely, caring, and funny girl. "Are you staying at mine tonight?" I asked her. "Well, I think I will go home, I have some things to do in the morning Liam" "Ok, no pressure, but you are more than welcome". Joan went home and I lay in my bed thinking about this beautiful girl but also feeling intrigued at why I had fallen so deeply in love with her. I had had many girlfriends but had never had these feelings before, maybe it was just that thing called love.

I was soon asleep and the dreams started again.

It was Sunday and we weren't awoken by the slave driver. I woke and asked Jankay why we weren't in work. "The master let's us have Sunday off to go to church. The master at the last place didn't, he worked us like dogs, but this Master seems better. They tell me each slave is given a small plot of land to grow food. I suggest me, you and Oday work together, that way we will produce more".

LOOKING FOR SHONA

That morning Grapes showed us the plots that the Master had said we could grow our food on. He kicked some soil at Oday and laughed, "Good luck growing anything in this" and he walked away. "That bastard, we will show him Oday". Our plots, luckily, were all together. We worked all day and then sat round a camp fire at night. One of the younger black slaves brought us some food. The food was dreadful but after toiling all day, beggars can't be choosers, as my mum used to say. Jankay and Oday laughed as the young girl brought me extra broth. "Why are you laughing?" "We all know why she is giving you extra young Cabhan" "Don't be daft" "You will see".

While we sat, I asked Jankay how he ended up a slave. He said he and Oday were brothers and had lived in St Kitts, he said they weren't rich but had a reasonably good life making fishing nets and mending boats. One day the pirates came he said they hid under one of the boats. The pirates collected all the men folk and three women and were about set off back to the main ship in their rowing boat, when Oday sneezed. They came back and found us, it must be almost three years now that we have been on this island, as slaves. "Why did the last master sell you both?" "After Oday had his tongue cut out, they said he was a trouble maker, the master said I would be no good without him so they sold us both and luckily we are still together".

After a hard day setting up the plots I felt tired. Although the bed was awful and you could hear all the critters, I did sleep well that night. As soon as it was light the Slave driver came barking out his orders, he then pulled me aside. "You go with her". This beautiful black girl took me by the hand, "You are coming to work at the house today. My name is Shona what is yours?" "Cabhan" "It will be better for you today Cabhan". Shona took me to the tradesmen's entrance and I was met by the butler, he said his name was Mr Tammy and I was to address him as such. He told me I was to work in the gardens and that I would be housed nearer the big house.

LOOKING FOR SHONA

Mr Tammy showed me to my room, which was much better than the rat infested hovel I had been in. He said I would be fed twice a day when the bell sounded. He seemed quite a nice man he was black, but very light in colour, I was guessing he was mixed race. He took me to the gardens and told me to weed this massive flowerbed, then I had to water the flowers every day and this would be my job from now on. I was grateful but thought about Jankay and Oday a lot, how dreadful for them.

You guessed at 3.30am I woke again with the dream clearly embedded in my mind. The beautiful Shona resembled my Joan so much, maybe this was just some kind of dream and not something I had lived. I phoned Jamie at 10.00am to see if he fancied a round of golf, Millie would often come but she said she was going shopping with her friend up the West End. Jamie wasn't a bad golfer for a wannabee Italian. By the ninth hole I was two over par and Jamie was eight over. "Looks like another easy fifty quid Jamie lad" "Time yet Egan" and he laughed. The back nine was disastrous for me and I ended up fifteen over. Jamie needed to sink his putt from twelve yards to beat me, which he duly did. You would think he had just won the Open. All course etiquette went out of the window as he ran round the green like a demented Banshee. "Pay up loser", he shouted. An elderly couple were getting quite agitated at Jamie's performance as they were waiting to play their shots. Eventually he calmed down and we walked back to the clubhouse. Jamie was telling anyone who would listen about England one Ireland nil. "Only as good as your last round Mr Egan" and he laughed milking it for all he was worth.

We ordered a champagne brunch at the clubhouse and we sat talking, with Jamie periodically stopping members to tell them he had won after nineteen attempts from when he last beat me.

"How is Glofachs? Have you heard?" "Millie saw Jayne yesterday and she said he was going to have life threatening surgery today Liam". "Bloody hell, poor bloke". "How are you and the lovely Miss Berry?" "Do you mean Joan Forde?" "Blimey must be serious for you if you know her surname, where does she live?" "I don't know she doesn't seem to want me to know. Perhaps she lives in a drug den in the East End!" and he laughed. "Well she certainly gives that impression, you prat Jamie" and they both laughed.

"I didn't want to ask you, but have the dreams gone away?" "No they are intensifying and I wake up at exactly 3.30am after them every time". "How weird Liam, why don't you do that regression thing it might help?" "To be honest, half of me wants it to stop and half of me wants to find things out Jamie". Then Liam told Jamie about Shona and how she looked like Joan. "It must just be a dream, you have met Joan and fitted her into your sub conscious in some way".

"When are you seeing Joan again?" "I think she doesn't want me to be pushy and she is a bit mysterious" "You don't think she is married do you?" "Bloody hell, I never thought of that Jamie. It's a possibility". "Liam she is a stunning woman, men would fall over themselves to be with her" "Oh that's right big her up and make me feel bad" and he laughed. "Come on, let go to Dick's Sports Bar and watch the Liverpool v Man Utd game". "I'm up for that" "Well Millie won't be back from town until tonight I bet, and you aren't seeing the beautiful mysterious Joan are you?"

They turned down into Shaftesbury Street and as if on cue they saw Joan with a black guy going into an Argentinean restaurant. "Bloody hell mate, did you just see what I saw?" Liam went, quiet but nodded. "Did you see the car she got out of? Only a bloody Ferrari F12 Berlinetta! That thing is a monster it has a 6:3 litre engine". Jamie was into cars so knew the make, model, engine size, you name it Jamie knew his cars. "Any wonder she didn't want you to see where she lived. Let's walk past and see if we can see him".

They walked slowly past the window, Joan wasn't at the table but the guy was.

"It's that boxer, Henry Manton; he holds all the belts in the middleweight division. Think you have blown that one old son" "Come on; let's get wasted at the sports bar". It was almost midnight when the pair staggered out of the bar to find a kebab shop. Finally after eating a big, greasy kebab, which you always regret the next day, they caught taxi. The taxi dropped Jamie off first and then Liam and he went into the flat and climbed into bed.

I was soon asleep and back into my slave world. The day spent in the garden was quite enjoyable, Shona would walk by, hanging washing out and each time she would smile. Suddenly as if I was in a Dr Who programme my life moved forward and I was now nineteen.

I was now working in the orchards tending the fruit and the vegetable gardens, I longed in my dream to see Shona but it was as if I had left her behind. I was plucking fruit from the trees when the Master came into the orchard.

"Cabhan we are pleased with your work. Are any of the indentured staff (they said indentured it was just posh for slaves) boat builders do you know?" I thought straight away of my friend's Jankay and Oday. I didn't look at the Master as that wasn't allowed, but I told him about Jankay and Oday but now I worked at the house I hadn't seen them for many years. "Oday is the mute isn't he and his brother is Jankay?" "Yes Sir" "Well thank you Cabhan. You may eat one of the apples you pick today, but only one mind" "Thank you Sir". I wanted to ask him about Shona but I daren't.

The Master was quite an old man now, he was dressed in a white linen suit with a cream shirt, he wore a big white hat and he had a cane with a golden eagles head on it. He was a little unsteady on his feet and as he neared the house, I watched he didn't fall over and then I started to eat my apple. The slave driver Coy was watching me from an upstairs window but I didn't know. I finished my apple and set about the pruning. Coy appeared. "Stealing were you boy?" "No Sir" "Don't lie to me, I saw you watch the old man and has soon as he had gone you ate one of his apples" "The Master told me to have an apple". "Well I don't believe you and he won't know what he's said, he forgets things. So I will be teaching you a lesson white boy, then I will string you up so the rest of them can see what happens when you steal".

Coy went for his bullwhip. I could no longer stand this punishment and I flipped out, I grabbed the bull whip and wrapped it round his neck and I choked him to death. I then dragged Coy's body to a pit I had dug, which was for all the rubbish we used to put it in and then we set fire to it, but I put the bastard in it and made good the ground. I knew at most I would have a day to get away before I was found out. I hid out for a day then the following morning I ran to the beach, my luck was in Oday and Jankay were working on the boats. I told Jankay what I had done. "We have no choice, if I give you the boat they will string us up" "Get in the boat Cabhan while we put holes in the others so they can't follow us" "We need to go now"

"Go where Jankay?" "Some of the other slaves have said there are more islands to the West, so we will follow the sun". Jankay and Oday wrecked the other boats and piled in the best remaining boat and set off with Cabhan. On their journey they managed to catch a few fish and ate them raw, they finally landed at another island after rowing for four day's taking turns to sleep. The islands, on first appearance, seemed deserted but we were soon to find this wasn't the case.

I woke from my dream feeling really thirsty and mouth tasted really fishy, what the bloody hell was happening with me? I decide later that day to phone Millie. Millie and Jamie asked me round to discuss what to do. I told them my dream and I was Cabhan and where I was capable of killing another human being. Where were these dreams taking me? "I saved the magazine Liam, the lady is called Nicola Gielbert, she is French apparently, and practises in Greenwich shall I phone now and make an appointment?" Liam hesitated for a minute. "Look Liam you can't go on like this" "I know you are right Millie, yes book it".

Millie picked up the phone and rang Nicola Gielbert. A very posh French accent answered the call. "Nicola Gielbert, how can I help you?". "Oh hi, I am calling on behalf of a friend, a Mr Liam Egan. Could I book a regression session with you for him?" "May I ask why he wants a regression session?" "He is having terrible dreams". "Ok, I see, well I have Thursday at 2.00pm free for a consultation". Millie looked at Liam "2.00pm Thursday Liam?" Liam nodded, "Yes that will be fine Nicola. Thank you he will see you then".

"Sorry to ask this Millie would you come with me?" "Actually it won't be a problem, I am off two days next week, the school is having a building inspection so I am off Thursday and Friday" "Sorry to be cheeky Jamie" "No worries mate, as long as once this is sorted you don't play golf any better than me, then I am more than happy". "Thank you, both of you" "Any time mate". "Now what are you going to do about Joan?" "What about Joan,

Liam?" "Hasn't Jamie told you? We saw her going into a restaurant with a boxer?" "Maybe they are friends, women can have male friends you know" "I know" "Look why don't you call her and see if you can meet up? If you don't, this will eat you up like your dreams" "Thanks Millie, I will think about it".

I left Jamie and Millie's and decided to call Joan and see if we could meet. Joan answered almost immediately. "Hi Liam, how are you?" "Good, thank you, been up to much?" "Just sorting something's out?" "When do you fancy meeting up again?" "Can I call you? Only I am in Switzerland with work on Monday, Tuesday and Wednesday, then I have a few meetings in Liverpool, so I will call you either Friday or Saturday". Liam was getting the impression he was getting the brush off. "Ok Joan I will wait for your call" and he ended the conversation. Typical he thought just when he thought he had got a nice relationship going, it just crumbled. He didn't expect to hear from Joan again.

Back home he watched a bit of TV then headed for bed. Funnily enough he didn't have anymore dreams before he went to see Nicola Gielbert on the Thursday. Liam picked up Millie and they arrived at her practise, spot on 2.00pm. "Don't be nervous Liam, you will be fine" "It's really weird, since you booked this consultation for me, I have had no more dreams" "Maybe that was all you needed Liam".

Nicola shook the hands of Millie and Liam then sat them down to explain what would be happening. "Right Liam, first of all I need to know why you feel regression is required" Millie stepped in. "Liam has been having terrible dreams and I saw an article about you, where you regressed a lady with the same problems and after regression she no longer had the dreams". "Mrs Egan, first of all let me explain" "Sorry, I am not Mrs Egan, I am a friend of Liam's" "Oh I am sorry, my mistake" "No problem".

"Regression involves taking the position of a child in some problematic situation, rather than acting in a more adult way. This is usually caused by some kind of stressful situations. The dreams you say you are having could be being triggered by stress at work or even in your private life. By regressing you we can hopefully find the trigger that is causing you anxiety and then address it accordingly. I am sorry if this sounds simplistic it certainly is not". "Before we start, do you fully understand what I am about to perform on you?" "Yes, thank you" "I will just need you to sign this form, giving me the right to carry out your regression". Liam duly signed the form. "You may come in, if you wish, Millie".

All three of them entered into quite a clinical room, there was soft soothing music playing and Liam was instructed to lie on the bed. Millie sat and watched. Just relax Liam we are going on a journey. Within seconds Liam was in some kind of trance. "What's your name Liam?" "Don't know" "I think you do Liam, try again". Liam hesitated then said "Cabhan".

"Where do you live Liam?" "Ireland"
"Sorry, say that again Cabhan" "Claw
Bay" Liam replied. "With your mother
and father?" asked Nicola. "No I live with
Jankay and Oday". "Who are Jankay and
Oday?" "My friends, they look after me".
Suddenly Liam started thrashing about as
if having some kind of fit. He was
shouting 'don't hurt me Mr Coy please
please'. As quickly as it started it stopped.
"Who is Mr Coy?" "I can't tell you"
"Why can't you tell me?" "Because they
will hunt me down and hang me" replied
Liam. "Who will?" "Them". "Who are
them?, Cabhan" continued Nicola. Liam
never answered. "Why won't you tell me
Cabhan?" "You might tell Shona". "Who
is Shona Cabhan?" Liam lay silent and
never answered anymore questions from
Nicola Gielbert.

Nicola turned to Millie. "I will bring him
out of regression slowly, now this may
take a few minutes so please don't panic,
he will be fine. Cabhan, can you come
back to me? Please, Liam needs you back
here". Liam's eyes flickered but he still
didn't stir this carried on for ten minutes.

Still Liam didn't come round. Millie could see Nicola was getting concerned as she kept trying to bring him back. After almost half an hour Liam eventually came round. He was a little dazed and confused at first, wanting to know why he was where he was. Millie explained but he still seemed confused. "Will he be ok?" "He will be fine Millie. I will get you both a coffee and a biscuit then he should be ok".

Millie felt that Liam still wasn't right as they left Gielbert's practise. Millie took Liam to a small coffee shop in Knightsbridge, one that they all used to go too thinking this may help him.

"I feel really weird" he said. "You do know who I am don't you Liam?" Liam looked at her strangely. "Are you my girlfriend?" Suddenly the enormity of what Millie had suggested about regression was starting to feel like a big mistake. She phoned Jamie and told him to finish work and get down to the coffee shop. Liam was asking Millie questions about gardening, which was weird as they lived in an apartment and she only had window boxes.

Come on Jamie she thought as they sipped their coffee. Jamie arrived in a panic. "What's up?" "Look at Liam" Liam was looking round in a daze. "Liam, its Jamie". "Hello Jamie, nice to meet you". "Bloody hell, his isn't good, we need to take him back".

They set off back to Nicola's practise she was just locking the door to leave for the night. "Hello is everything ok?" "It's a long way short of ok, Liam doesn't know anyone and he is in a daze". Nicola took them into the practise. "I will be honest with you. I have never seen such a troubled soul as Liam. He has massive underlying memories the only thing I can do is regress him again and try again". "What do you bloody mean the only thing you can do, are you saying if this doesn't work we have lost Liam forever?" "Please don't swear at me, everyone knew the risk it was fully explained to Mr Egan and I will do my best, but one session clearly isn't going to be enough. Please calm down because stress does not help Liam".

Nicola put Liam on the bed again and regressed him. "Cabhan?" "Yes" Liam replied "Don't you want to come back to Liam?" Suddenly he spoke again but his accent was broad Irish. "I need to find Shona and they are looking for me" "Who are looking for you?" "Morton's men" "Who is Mr Morton?" "My owner", replied Liam. Jamie sat listening to this, it seemed incredible. "I didn't steal honestly" "I am sure you didn't Cabhan, now come back to Liam, he is waiting". Liam never replied but slowly came round. "Jamie what are you doing here/". Jamie could have cried he hugged his best mate. Millie was crying. "Why are you all upset? I thought I was going to have this treatment done" "You have Liam you should be ok now". "What did I say?" "Nothing, but you have inner peace now". Before he had come round Nicola had instructed Jamie and Millie not to discuss with Liam what he had said under regression as it may trigger the situation they had seen after the first regression.

They thanked Nicola and she said it maybe that I would need further sessions but she felt she could address my anxiety. "How come you came Jamie?" "I was a bit quiet at work, so thought I would come and support you mate" "Did I say anything?" "Not sure mate me and Millie were told to sit outside" "Hope you didn't give her your bank details" and Jamie laughed. "Shall we go for a meal? Do you know for some reason I fancy something Caribbean". Millie looked at Jamie. "Don't you like Caribbean food Millie? If not we can go somewhere else". Jamie was mindful what Nicola had said so he made out he fancied a burger and Millie agreed. "Ok burger it is then. Let's go to Big Al's they have cracking burgers there". Big Al's was very busy but they found a seat near the window. A waitress in pigtails, flared skirt and bobby socks came to take the order the restaurant was styled on Happy Days and the Fonz. The waiters and waitress, as soon as Happy Days theme tune was played by the DJ, stopped what they were doing and danced on the bar. It was quite a fun place.

Jamie ordered the Blackened burger with curly fries, Millie ordered the Chilli Burger with curly fries and Liam ordered the Nashville burger with beer battered fries. "So mate, did you speak with Joan?" "Yeah she said she was out of the country until Wednesday, then in Liverpool and back Friday. She would call me either on Friday or Saturday" "That's good then mate" "Not really, I get the impression she is giving me the brush off" "Wait until next weekend, then you will know" "Don't see it, if she was interested she could have seen me this weekend". Anyway plenty more fish as they say. Millie thought it was good Liam hadn't mentioned anything about his dreams maybe Nicola Gielbert had sorted it for him.

The burgers arrived they were massive Millie could not believe that anyone could eat one, it was like that programme Man vs Food. Although Liam was ok, both Jamie and Millie thought he was not at his best when they dropped him at his apartment. "Give me a call over the weekend Liam" "Yes, will do". Liam disappeared into his apartment.

"He isn't right Jamie "I can see that, but what do we do" "You will have to keep a close eye on him and if need be we take him back to Nicola for another session. How can all this have happened after a drunken Ouija board game? I wish we had never played it" "Well I bet Liam does"
.

Liam made himself a milky coffee. Feeling tired he fell asleep. The dreams started again. "Jankay where are we?" "I think we are in St Vincent, but I'm not sure". The island seemed deserted. "I'm not sure we can stay, they know we rowed away and they will come after us Cabhan" "First we need to find some fresh water then get some sleep". There was an abundance of fresh water and fruit on the island once they were full they lay down for the night.

The sunrise had begun when they were woken by the dreaded Mr Grapes with four big burly Slave Drivers. "What have we here? The thief, the mute and the fool.

Manacle them boys, you are going home to a fate you can't imagine". All three men were dragged by their feet to the waiting boats then taken back to Barbados. They arrived back near the big house.

"Put the mute against the tree and tie his arms round it and take off his shirt. Grab the other two and ensure they watch". This British man then started whipping poor Oday because he couldn't speak, all we could here were muted noises from him. Jankay turned to Grapes "Let him go, I will take the lashings" "You are too valuable Mr Jankay, its market for you" "I will take the lashings" "The Bog Arab speaks" and Grapes laughed, "You young Cabhan, are to be summoned in front of the Master he has something special for you". Grapes carried on whipping Oday until he passed out. His back was so badly lacerated there was blood everywhere. "Do you all see now?" Grapes said, the gathering slaves all looked terrified. "If you run away or are disobedient, then this will be your peril. Get me a rope", Grapes barked to one of the Slave drivers. They put a noose on it and then hauled poor

Oday up in the air and left him choking to death. He was already unconscious; hopefully his pain will be less.

"Take Mr Jankay, clean him up, clean his teeth and get him ready for market tomorrow. Cabhan, you come with me" "Goodbye my friend" "Goodbye Jankay, I am so sorry, I will find you one day and that I promise". Jankay looked at him his eyes like pearls in a dark place. I will never forget this day I thought and Grapes will pay. As he dragged me to the big house I kept thinking about Coy they could not have found him or I would be in the tree with Oday. Mr Grapes took me into this massive room all decorated with paintings and lavish furniture. Humphrey Slaley Morton appeared. "Now then young Cabhan, where have you been?" I could not tell him what had happened or they will know I killed Mr Coy. "I wasn't running away Sir, I just wanted to look round" "Those two evil slaves talked you into it then Cabhan?" I just nodded and then immediately felt dreadful, I had betrayed my friends, one of which lost his life to help me.

LOOKING FOR SHONA

"Stand up boy, I want you to meet one of the kitchen girls her name is Shona". They had dressed Shona in some fine clothes she looked so beautiful. "You and Shona are going to make a baby for the house". Cabhan didn't know what to say. "Once Shona is with child you will never see her again. The child will be brought up as a new breed of slave and you Cabhan will go as an apprentice joiner to learn a trade".

I could not believe what I was hearing or seeing but there was not a choice we were taken to a room and told to breed by the Slave Driver his last words were 'and hurry up'. It was lucky that clearly we were both attracted to each other. I fumbled about, it was my first time and Shona said it was hers, she was seventeen and I was nineteen. I don't think either of us was impressed, but we had to do as we were told. As soon as we finished the Slave Trader had been watching and laughing. He grabbed me by the arm and I was led away.

He took me down to the Joiners shop. I was presented to the Joinery Master a Mr James Wilson he seemed ok but then he assigned me to a tradesman a man named William Miller. William Miller was a tall man about six foot three he wore a brown smock and was very tidy. He had long dark hair and was not a black or a white but somewhere in-between. The first thing he did was show me a piece of carved wood he said it was Iroko and was a very hardwood, it was about three inches thick with spiked barbs on it. Mr Miller said if ever I step out of line he would hit me with this because I would deserve it. Then he said, "Do you believe in God boy?" "Yes I do", I said. "Then you will come to Church with me twice on a Sunday, once at 11.00am and once at 5.00pm" I nodded remembering what my dear friend Jankay had told me about surviving and not to look at the Master.

"Right this is where you will eat and sleep. I will give you two meals a day if you leave any food then I will cut you down to one meal a day understood". "Yes Sir". He grabbed me by my ear and said. "You boy call me Mr Miller" "Yes Mr Miller" I repeated and he let go. "You will start work at sunrise and will finish work at sunset not a minute later. The Master at the great house has been good to you so make sure you repay him". And he left me to sort out my bed.

The room was about six feet by six feet, the bed was a wooden one with straw for bedding. At least I could not hear any rats, "bet they are frightened of Mr Miller" I thought, I know I certainly was. I lay on the bed thinking about Shona and that I was possibly a father. My mind wandered to my two friends and poor Oday. Jankay would be fine he was a survivor and one day I vowed to find him. Hopefully I would find Shona and my child one day and escape, then I would find Jankay and release him from slavery. This wood working thing maybe my only escape route. I just prayed that they didn't find Coy.

Things started to blur and I woke up. Millie was next to me holding my hand there was a bright light above me and I thought I was in hospital, but I had been in regression.

I started to remember being in a Burger bar with Millie and Jamie, then going home and making a milky coffee, but after that nothing. Nicola Gielbert had made me a coffee and we sat on the chintzy settee. "Millie what happened to me?" "You didn't make work Liam. Jamie phoned me so I came round to check on you. The door was open and you were sat on the settee crying" "Really? did I say why?" "You just kept saying, 'Shona and poor Oday'. I called Nicola and she told me to just bring you immediately to the practise so I did". Nicola then spoke. "Liam I regressed you and you went even further back. I have been doing this for many years and have never seen such a deep underlying problem in any patient" "What does that mean Nicola?" "It means, I am sorry but we are on a journey into the unknown. What I want you to do is if you have any flashback or any more dreams you must call me or come in immediately. I don't want to frighten you but with you losing days from your memory this can be very serious Liam".

Millie and Liam finished their coffee and thanked Nicola and Liam assured her if there was a problem he would contact her immediately. They walked through Knightsbridge and onto Canary Wharf. "Are you going to be ok Liam?" "Yes I will be fine, I am going to go in and see Jenny Fenney. I don't want to lose my job" "Are you going to tell her?" "I'm not sure yet".

Liam left Mille at the entrance to work and went inside. Jamie was busy so he went straight to Jenny's office. "Oh, hello Liam pleased you could make it" "Jenny let me explain". Before he could say anything more Jenny started her rant. "Liam do not take our social friendship in the wrong context. While you are at work I expect one hundred percent from you. I expect you here, at work, on time and trading when the bell goes, that is expected from all of you under my supervision". Liam tried to intervene but Jenny was in full flow. "I don't know if you are using, but if you are you need to stop. You are a good trader, but I will have no qualms about releasing you if this nonsense carries on. Do I make myself clear?" I knew trying to explain to Jenny wasn't an option, so I took it on the chin. "I expect you back at work tomorrow and trading when the bell goes at 9.00am" "Ok Jenny, I won't let you down" "I want to believe that Liam".

I left the office feeling dreadful. My boss thinks I am taking drugs and has lost faith in me. How the hell do I address this? I gestured to Jamie to meet him at 6.00pm at Molly Malone's Irish Bar in Fellow Street.

Jamie arrived a half hour late so I was on my second Guinness. "Hey mate how are you? Saw Jenny giving you a dressing down" "It's really bad, Jenny thinks I am taking drugs or something because I missed work". "What?? Surely not mate, do you want me to have a word??" "No leave it Jamie, it will look like I am hiding something".

"Look mate, I know this is tough but me and Millie will get you through this have a few beers it will help you sleep and now I know the score give me a key and I will call each morning on the way to work to make sure nothing went wrong in the night" "Jamie you are a star mate, I don't know what I would do without you".

A good few beers later and Liam spotted one of the girls Joan was with at the nightclub that night. "Hey how are you?". The girl looked at Liam like he was a space man. "Do you not remember me?" "Sorry I don't know you". Liam tried again. "You are Joan's friend aren't you?" Again the girl reeled back. "Look I don't know who you are or what your game is, but I'm not interested". Jamie pulled Liam away. "You were there that night Jamie" "I have to say Liam I am pretty sure she was with Joan. I remember that girl had a strawberry birth mark on her upper leg and unless they are identical twins she does".

"There is something odd going on here Jamie" "Look mate maybe Joan isn't interested just accept it". The night ended with Liam even more confused. "Why would somebody pretend they didn't know Joan?" "Just accept she isn't interested Liam" "Jamie there is more to this than just a boyfriend girlfriend thing". Jamie looked at Liam but didn't comment. His mate was losing the plot.

Almost three months passed and Liam had heard nothing from Joan so he assumed that was over. He had had no more dreams, so had told Nicola Gielbert the situation and she was confident that he would no longer get the dreams. Jenny Fenney seemed a lot better with Liam, his work and concentration had improved. All seemed rosy in the garden.

Another two months passed, I had no further dreams or heard from Joan so assumed now that she wasn't interested. London was very busy at this time of year so I decided to take a break. I asked my friend Jayne Tupton if she fancied a cruise for two weeks. I had been friends with Jayne through our University years and we were just that, good friends. She was at a loose end so she agreed.

My life felt good again and a perfect time to take a well-earned break. Jenny Fenney was impressed with my figures and I had made a sizeable bonus, so said I would treat Jayne. Jayne worked at a publishing house, which wasn't particularly great money, she had to do like an apprenticeship and it would be five years before she would start to earn what I considered a good wage.

With everything booked we flew to Puerto Rico for our cruise. The cruise took in St Kitts, Guadeloupe, Lucia and finally Barbados. I know what you must be thinking, Barbados? But I felt good that everything was done with regard to Cabhan, so I felt good about it. Although I did phone Nicola Gielbert to see what she thought? Nicola said she was a little apprehensive, but she was always here if the dreams came back and that I couldn't let it ruin my life.

LOOKING FOR SHONA

The first two nights were spent in a beautiful hotel The La Concha Renaissance Hotel in San Juan Resort. On arrival we were met with two of the largest cocktails you could imagine. They had more fruit in them than Waitrose have on their shelves. "This is fantastic Liam, thank you for bringing me". "Not a problem Jayne, I must owe you a fortune the amount of times you cooked for me in that flippin bedsit we shared". "Good day's hey Liam?" "They certainly were. Do you remember Jack Webster who shared with us? He would never wash his pots" "Yeah and he had the habit of passing wind and then leaving the room, so if we had people round the smell would linger". Liam started to laugh. "Good lad though, I wonder what happened to him?" "I have him as a Facebook friend, he lives in Cornwall and runs a bar with a girl down there" "Well that's about right Jayne, he always was a piss head". "I'm going up to freshen up Liam; shall we meet in the lobby for about 7.00pm and then find somewhere nice to eat?" "Sound's like a plan".

Liam went back to his room, it was very palatial, the king size bed had been adorned with swans made from towels, there were flowers on the large oval table in the sitting room area and a bowl of fresh fruit. Double doors led to a patio area with a personal hot tub and sun lounger. 'This is beautiful', he thought.

Liam fell asleep and woke just before 7.00pm, he quickly showered and changed and ran down to the lobby. Jayne was laughing, "Never on time Egan, nothing changes" "Sorry Jayne, you look great". Jayne had a long flowing white dress with a small sun hat, which had small cloth flowers round the edges. "Come on Smoothy Pants, let's head into town" "How far to the nearest restaurants please?". The polite girl behind the desk indicated about a thirty minute walk. They set off, there was a cool breeze but it was still over 30c as they finally arrived at a cluster of restaurants situated on and around the beach area.

"This looks like a nice spot Jayne, shall we try it?" "Yeah great Liam, what a fabulous name for a restaurant too" "I know The Renaissance Tapestry sounds great". They were greeted by a smiling waiter who took their coats and showed them to their table overlooking the beach and the sea.

"This is wonderful Liam, thank you" "Any time mate, you know that". They ordered their meals, Jayne went for a small Asopao which was similar to a Gumbo soup, Liam had the same. Jayne followed that with traditional Lechon, which was suckling pig with all the trimmings, and Liam ordered the Monfongo. They ate their food and admired the view. "That was lovely Liam, how did you know what to order? Have you been before?" Liam suddenly realised that he did know what to order, how strange.

"I need to tell you something Jayne" "Oh? Not too serious I hope?" Liam told Jayne the full story. Jayne was a little shocked. "So ever since that night, you have had the dreams?" "Up until two months ago" "And who is Joan? Was she in the dreams then?" "You are going to think I am weird, but I met Joan in Sticky Vickie's. Me and Jamie went there, you know how Jamie loves to dance. Jamie went dancing and this stunning black girl came to talk to me. I couldn't believe my luck she was gorgeous". "So you went out with her?" "Yes a couple of times" "Did you sleep with her?" "Just the once and I have never seen her again" "She was impressed then Liam" and Jayne laughed. "Sorry only joking". "Thing is she seems to be in my dreams Jayne somehow". Just then the waiter interrupted them, "Excuse me Sir, we are closing now". "Shall we walk back across the sand?" asked Jayne "Yes why not", said Liam. The sand was pearly white and the full moon flooded the bay leaving what resembled a footpath to infinity across the water.

They arrived back at the hotel and they both had a Cognac for a night cap. Jayne thanked Liam again and went off to her room. Liam sat talking with the barman. "Filay, what a nice name" "Why thank you Sir" "Call me Liam" "Ok Liam" said the barman. "Well listen Filay, I will have a beer with you in the morning, before we leave for the ship" "I will look forward to it Sir, sorry Liam". Liam arrived back at his room and crashed on the bed, he was so full he thought he was going to burst. It wasn't long before he was in a deep sleep. The dreams started again. It was funny, because they nearly always started where they left off.

William Miller was a hard task master and on this day I cut a piece of wood wrong, the other boys all laughed and Miller went ballistic. "Come here boy". He told me to strip off and then he sat me across a weird contraption and tied my arms to the legs. Next he got out a whip. It was made up of leather straps with knots along the full length of the straps. Each strap was about two metres long and there were twelve of them.

Miller stood over me and said "Are you sorry boy?" I said "Yes" "Will you cut my wood wrong again boy?" "No Sir" I said. "Do you know I am going to punish you boy" "Yes Sir" "Am I right to punish you boy?". I had seen one boy question Miller at this point and he'd beaten him within an inch of his life, so I knew I had to say I deserved a whipping. "I deserve a whipping Sir". Miller started whipping me, I counted every stroke, and there were twelve before he stopped. Then he rubbed salt into my wounds. Bizarrely he thanked me for my forgiveness. I hated him, but could not show that. They stood me up and I felt woozy, he then told me to carry on working. How I wish I could have hit him, but that would have meant certain death. Suddenly I woke it was at the usual time of 3.30pm, but I didn't know why my back felt sore, there were no marks and it was just a little red. I lay there just totally confused again.

It was soon 9.00am; the time I said I would meet Jayne for breakfast. "Liam have you seen all this food?" The hotel's breakfast could have fed an army it was fabulous in the extreme. Liam sat there in a bit of a daze. "You ok Liam?" "Look Jayne I have to tell you something about me" "Ok, this sounds ominous Liam, more dreams?"

"Remember the night at your flat when we played Ouija on my birthday?" Jayne laughed, "Yeah and Jamie was pushing the glass at you and the name Cob or something came out?" "Yes, the name was Cabhan. Since that night I have dreamt I was an Irish slave living in Barbados" "What? Are you kidding me?" "I wish I was Jayne. I have been for regression treatment and the dreams stopped, but last night they started again. The girl in the UK called Joan, I took her out a few times but then she liked disappeared as if she never existed" "So she didn't fall for your charm then?" Jayne didn't say anything but Jamie had told her about Joan. "It's serious Jayne, it's really messing my life up. In the dream I meet a black girl called Shona and they make us mate, for the want of a better word". Jayne started to laugh. "I'm sorry Liam, but do you know how this sounds?" "Crazy I guess, but this girl Shona was the image of Joan" "Joan the mystery woman?" "Yes". "It's just a dream Liam your mind is playing tricks and I think you are fitting people into the dreams". "Well explain the regression sessions then.

Apparently I speak like I am from southern Ireland my name is Cabhan and I am a slave or indentured servant as they called them".

"Well you've certainly entertained me for the last hour. Who else have you told?" she asked, "Just you, Jamie and Millie. Millie went with me to the Regression therapy". "I like Millie she is a nice girl. What does she think?" "She has been really good with me. She has been at the regression sessions and I think, like you, at first she just thought they were dreams but she believes differently now".

"Ladies and Gentlemen, your coaches are ready for your cruise to St Kitts. You will have about six hours there to do your own thing. Entertainment tonight on the cruise include the seventies pop group Smokey. We also have a magician and a hypnotist. Dinner will be served at 7.00pm tonight. If you would like to make your way to the coaches please".

Liam and Jayne got on the first coach to the cruise liner. A magnificent ship stood in the dock it was so big it dwarfed the islands port. They climbed the gang plank and were greeted by the crew welcoming them aboard. They were given a small disc each which allocated their room and was to be used when ordering drinks and meals.

"I am in 513 with an Ocean view Liam". I am in 673 also Ocean view which I booked for us" "This is so nice of you Liam". Liam left Jayne at her door and carried on down the deck until he eventually arrived at his room 673. On entering he had a bathroom, wet room and toilet a beautiful study which led onto a balcony. He opened the fridge to see if there was a cold beer available and there was. He poured himself a glass of cold beer and sat on the balcony. 'This is the life he thought' and the ship had set off. You could hardly tell you were on water it was so smooth.

Liam had arranged to see Jayne in the lobby at 8.00pm for dinner. He relaxed on the balcony until 7.00pm then showered and changed into his tuxedo for dinner.

Jayne was waiting. She had on a long burgundy dress and with being so tall she carried the dress very well. Jayne complemented the dress with gold shoes and a gold clutch handbag. "You look stunning Jayne" "You don't look so bad yourself Mr Bond", the referencing being the tuxedo.

The evening meal was a seven course banquet. Liam managed all seven courses but Jayne struggled and missed a couple out. "I will be like a house side if I carry on eating like this Liam" "Just enjoy it" he said. Suddenly Liam went quiet. "Are you ok Liam? You have gone really pale". "Yeah sorry, you are going to think I am stupid but the big black guy serving the wine, he looks like somebody in the dreams. His name was Oday and he was a mute". "Well actually Liam, I do think you are nuts! You need to relax". Jayne called the waiter over and asked for another glass of wine. The waiter duly poured the wine but didn't speak, just nodded. "What wine do you have?" asked Liam. The waiter looked a little embarrassed and turned to another waiter and did some kind of sign language. The second waiter came across and tried to sort Liam out. "I am sorry, is your friend new? I didn't mean to embarrass him" "No nothing like that Sir, he hasn't been able to talk since he was born. We have been friends for ever so I understand his sign language". John dropped his fork. "Are you ok Sir" asked the waiter as he bent to pick up the fork. "Sorry yes, I'm fine thanks".

"Listen Jayne, I think I will make my way back to the room, I feel a bit shattered" "Liam what is the matter?" "The deaf, black guy looks like Oday in the dreams and he was a mute". "It's just a coincidence Liam you have to relax" "I know but do you mind if I call it a night?" "No go on" "We disembark for St Kitts at 10.00am, so shall we meet for breakfast at 8.30am Jayne?. "Ok see you then, sleep well and try and relax" "I will" and Liam disappeared out of the restaurant and up the deck to his room.

Once inside his room he broke down. 'What the hell is happening to me?' he thought. He showered again, made himself a coffee and took out his Kindle. Liam had been reading an autobiography on a former inmate of Alcatraz, Johnny Lincoln. Lincoln had been a bad ass. He had robbed banks across America in the early fifties, finally getting caught just outside Beatrice, Nebraska by a local cop Sergeant Al Kruger. He had wrestled Lincoln to the floor as he had fled the bank. Kruger was shot in the leg for his troubles but he hung onto Lincoln until back up arrived. Liam had found the book interesting and one day hoped to go to Alcatraz.

It was calm on the boat, Liam was soon asleep and same as last night the dreams started again.

Back in the woodwork shop, I could not lie on my back, it hurt so much. One of the other boys brought me a mix of coconut oil and mango juice he said older slaves had told him that would take the sting out of the wounds and would help the healing process. My new friends name was Lomo, he told me he was a son of a slave and didn't know anything other than where he had been brought up on the plantation. Lomo was about twenty three years old, he told me he would be able to work on his own in about two years' time. "You need a friend in here Cabhan, to show you the ropes or you won't last, Miller is a sadist, he enjoys bullying and whipping boys. Never cut a piece of wood without first measuring it, at least twice, remember that Cabhan".

"Can I tell you a secret?" "What Lomo?" "I have a girl her names is Aoi" "How do you say that?" "Drop the A it's Oo I" "How do you see each other?" "Well because I only have two years of my apprenticeship to do, I get more freedom. She works in the laundry. One day we are going to be married. Do you have a girlfriend Liam?" "No they told me I had to mate with a black girl her name was Shona" "I know Shona she is very pretty" "How do you know her?" "She works in the laundry, she had a baby but it was still born so the Master said she was barren and was to work in the steam of the laundry". "When you next go to see your

94

Aoi, will you tell her to speak with Shona and tell her I ask after her please Lomo?" "Of course now get some sleep don't tell anyone what I told you Cabhan".

The next morning we were woken at 4.00am, it was still a little dark so something else was the reason we were told to get up and stand in the yard. In the yard to my horror Mr Grapes stood with his bull whip in his hand.

"Right you barrel load of rats, today the body of a dear friend was found in the plantation garden by the dogs. Mr Coy has been strangled and one of you son's of bitches have done it. I know of five people that are standing here today that could have done it, they all had the opportunity. Step forward Abram". A small black kid stepped forward, he peed himself as he did so, and he was so frightened. Now Badru, a much bigger guy, who looked about thirty stood upright. Next Cilitoe, again he was another big black guy. Two more were to be shouted forward. I was waiting for my name but it never came out as he said "Step forward Criff and Hendon.

Which one of you killed Mr Coy?" Nobody said they did. "Ok this is what we will do. Badru will fight Cilitoe, Abram will fight Hendon and Criff will fight one of you that are left. The three that die were guilty, the three that live will get a big meal". I decided seeing that it was I that killed Coy, I should fight for the right to live, so I put my hand up. Grapes laughed "The Big Bog Arab fancies a slap up meal, hey well why not". The first two fights didn't last long Badru killed Cilitoe, then Abram killed Hendon. Criff was about the same size as me. It was a bit like handbags at fifty paces but I winded him. Dad always said wind your opponent, then their head will drop, and then you can knock them out. I did just that and poor Criff fell to the floor. I grabbed his neck and yanked it to one side snapping his neck. That was it. Grapes stood and laughed as they took the bodies away, he then instructed his men to throw each the survivors a piece of rotten fruit each. "There you go lads enjoy your meal" and he walked away laughing.

Nobody said anything, we daren't, but I learnt that night how to survive. I felt bad that the other men had lost their lives for what I had done, but it was dog eat dog, if I was to survive. I worked all day until dusk, my back was still sore and sadly I hadn't given a thought to the fellow slave I had killed. When I eventually climbed into bed I reflected on what I had become and how much I hated these people. My hope now was I would one day see Shona that was all I was living for.

It was almost three weeks before Lomo and I had the chance to speak, we were both sent to market with a chest of drawers we had made. Mr Grapes with one of his overseers, me and Lomo drove the thirty miles or so into town. The town was a ramshackle set of buildings, made of wood with tin rooves. All the white faces were those of well-dressed men with their slaves in tow, ready to be sold. It was market day. Slaves were sold like pieces of meat. The market also sold furniture, which was why we had come to town. Mr Grapes told us to get the chest of drawers off the cart and stand with it, if anybody asked how much the drawers were, we were to run and fetch them from a bar at the end of the street. Quite a few people looked at them but nobody asked a price.

"Cabhan, I spoke with Shona she said she would like to see you". I felt so excited, "How do I do that?" "Tonight would be best, Mr Grapes and the Overseer will be drunk and they will pass out. So it's easy". "Lomo, I am so excited, is she ok?" "She is, but I think the Master will take her for his pleasure". Cabhan could feel the hairs go up on the back of his neck. That slobbering old fool with his Shona, the thought disgusted him, how could he stop that happening?

Eventually a very well dressed man came and looked at the furniture. He was ignorant and barked at me "Hey white boy, how much for the chest of drawers?". I turned to Lomo, "Run and ask Mr Grapes". It seemed like ages before Grapes and the overseer came back, the man was about to leave, but I managed to talk him into staying if I hadn't me and Lomo would have been whipped. "Hello

Sir, the furniture is yours for a two King James shillings, Sir". The man didn't quibble, but paid for it, so we loaded it on his cart. "Get on the cart you two" shouted the Overseer.

On the way back they were laughing, saying how they would give the Master just one shilling because he would not remember and they would keep one shilling to share. They were so drunk in the end Lomo took the reins. We arrived back as the sun was setting and they went off to bed. "They really don't know where they are, do they Lomo?" "Not just now Cabhan, but we still have to be careful once they have slept it off".

"Come on quickly Cabhan". Cabhan followed Lomo into a cellar, down a lot of dark corridors until eventually they came into a room, it was quiet, but there was a lot of steam and sheets drying everywhere. From behind one of the sheets my beautiful Shona appeared just like a vision. I stood there in mis-belief. Eventually my feelings got the better of me and I held her, then I kissed her. She was the sweetest most beautiful thing I had ever seen.

Lomo was with his girl so I sat with Shona. She spoke quite good English, she told me she carried our baby for eight months, then one night the baby was born prematurely but they told her the baby was still born. She said it was a little girl and that they took the baby away. She had called her Alice, but never knew whether they were lying to her or not, as another slave had told her that they had done the same thing to her. My emotions again got the better of me and tears rolled down my rugged face. Shona put her arms round me and kissed me. "One day you will have served your apprenticeship and you will be given your freedom. Will you take me with you that day?" she asked. "I'm not sure I can wait that long Shona" he replied. "Listen to me Cabhan, if you cause any trouble the Master will sell you, then I will never see you again you must behave, we can get through this" "I know Shona, but I want to be with you so much". "Now you are going to market, Mr Grapes will take you every time if he

100

trusts you" said Shona. "Come on Cabhan, we must go" Lomo whispered. "I will see you soon my dearest" he kissed Shona. That night all he could think about was how he could escape this hell and take his Shona with him.

Suddenly Liam woke it was exactly 3.30am again, but this time the dream was very vivid. He tried to go back to sleep but it seemed after 3.30am the dreams stopped and he wanted to be back with Shona. He couldn't tell Jayne anymore, she would think he was nuts so he decided to enjoy the holiday and not mention his dreams again well certainly not to Jayne.

Liam met Jayne in the lobby and they had breakfast together. "You should have stayed last night Liam, the group were good and the hypnotist was brilliant" "What time did you stick it until Jayne?" "I think it was 2.45am when I climbed in bed". Liam was thinking he was with Shona at about that time. "Anymore dreams Liam?" "No, I think you are right, I just need to relax" "At last you silly thing" "I know Jayne, just that bloody Ouija board game really spooked me!"

The passengers were let onto the quay side and were told that they had until 8pm that night before the cruise ship would sail. It was now 11.00am so they had a good nine hours on land. There were many people trying to sell Island tours they decided to take one. A pleasant island guide started telling them the history of the island and the first stop was the capital Basseterre. The capital had a very strong English and French influence through the years. They were given four hours to wander the town before the coach picked them up for the next leg of the tour.

"Liam, quick, look at this". Jayne was bent down at the roadside where a small stone had carvings shaped into it. It depicted a slave hanging. Below the carved picture was a date 1634 in the reign of Charles 1st. There was some other lettering but with time they had all but disappeared. Liam thought he could see an L and an M but it wasn't clear. Liam said he felt sick. "You had too much breakfast?" asked Jayne. "It's not that Jayne, something in my head is telling me who carved the stone". "Oh Liam, not that again". "Sorry, just me being silly. Let's have a drink in this little bar on the beach".

The bar was only small, it would have probably only had seating for twelve or fifteen people and about the same outside. The roof was made of tin with palm leaves covering it. The deck outside was right on the beach. "This is fabulous Liam, look at the sand and the water, it's so clear". "I wish I had brought my swimming trunks Jayne" "Eeeewwww no! I've heard about your budgie smugglers" and she laughed.

Liam turned to the barman, "Can we have two St Kitts cocktails please?" "Certainly Sir, please take a seat I will bring them to you". They chose to sit outside. The barman arrived with two strange shaped glasses. The cocktail was green for the first quarter of the glass, then red, then orange and finally blue. On the top was pineapple, orange, mango and then it was sprinkled with coconut and finished off with an umbrella and a sparkler. "Thank you. Blimey Liam it will take a fortnight to drink this, there is at least bowl of fruit in it" and she laughed.

They relaxed and chatted, Liam avoided any further conversation about his dreams, but he kept wondering why he seemed to know so much about the roadside carving. The four hours flew by and the next stop was Brimstone Hill National Park. The guide, a small lady, in the tour company suit started to explain. "Hi my name is Lucy, I hope you had a nice stop-over in Basseterre and hopefully had a famous St Kitts cocktail?" A big cheer went up on the coach. "On the way we will stop at a very important place in the history of St Kitts. This was the scene, in 1626, where the French and the English massacred the Caribbean and Arawak people, at this the Pelham River, known from that day as the bloody river. This was the ceremonial meeting place of these people and they were systematically murdered that day for the gain of the French and the English. To this day, native St Kitts's people still harbour a grudge for what happened to their people".

"This must have been some scary place in those days" said Liam. "Yeah, I agree Jayne". Liam knew the islands well but didn't want to mention all that to Jayne again.

The rep continued, "The Island was then split between the French and the English. The French took the outer ends of the island and the English took the middle they shared the South East Peninsula with its salt ponds, between them. This was never going to be a long term relationship and in 1629 the first armed conflict on St Kitts happened between the two countries. A few months after that conflict, a large Spanish fleet captured the islands. They were a force to be reckoned with in those days".

The next part of the reps story, Liam felt an enormous amount of déjà vu. The rep started the story of how, in 1639, the slaves revolted. They were mainly French slaves. They waged a guerrilla war from the foot hills of Mount Misery but were eventually and ruthlessly crushed by the French Governor Philippe de Poincey.

Liam could feel his whole body shaking and he began to sweat. "Are you ok Liam?" asked Jayne" "I'll be ok, I wonder if I have picked up a bug". Jayne passed him a bottle of water and as he drank it seemed to calm Liam's body down.

"Right everybody, if you would all like to leave the coach, starting at the front. You must all be back at the coach no later than 6.00pm for our journey back to the ship please".

Jayne and Liam left the coach and climbed some very old and well-worn stone steps, leading all the way to the Fortress. This was a very impressive piece of Island history. Jayne was in her element, she loved all the history stuff but Liam was finding things quite tough, due to the dreams but he soldiered on.

The area easily took up the time allocated by the tour operator, so Jayne and Liam wandered back to the coach, almost being the last ones to get on. You know how you feel when you arrive late? Everyone was looking at them, as they took their seats on the coach. "Keep your head down Egan, I think a few are not happy with us almost being late" "We are actually spot on time by my watch Jayne!!"

"Well that was a lovely day Liam, who would have thought all those years ago, when we met as young spotty kids, that we would both be living in London and holidaying together on these beautiful islands?". "I know you have to pinch yourself, hey Jayne?" "Do you remember our first year in the halls of residence and you fancied the pants of my room-mate Siobhan Reilly? You said she looked like a younger Demi Moore out of that film Ghost with Patrick Swayze" "Oh yeah, what happened to her do you keep in touch?" "Yeah, she dropped out halfway through her final year said she'd had enough of schooling. She is married now with two kids, lives in Bromsgrove. She has got a shop that sells arty farty stuff. She was always into that". "I never did get to take her out" said Liam. "Probably the only one that didn't fall for that Irish charm me thinks" "Give over Jayne" and Liam laughed.

"Look I could do with an hour to freshen up Liam; shall we meet down here about 9.30pm and just have something light to eat? They have got Bingo on at ten, shall we have a go?" "You are still flippin' adventurous Jayne!".

They both went to their respective rooms showered and were back down in the lobby by 9.30am. "What do you fancy to eat Jayne?" "Not a lot actually. Shall we have just a Mexican starter or small portion?" "Ok that sounds good to me". They wandered over to the Mexican buffet, which was enormous. Liam had a Chile Poblanos and Jayne tried the Burrito.

With their food now consumed, they headed for the Bingo. "Can't believe I am playing Bingo Jayne" "Come on you will enjoy it", she giggled. The compare on the stage was really camping it up. He had on a bright blue jacket, covered in sequins, and he had bright blonde hair. "Good evening everybody, thank you for joining us tonight for Housey Housey Bingo. I am your compare, my name is Jez and my lovely assistants are Becky, take a bow love, Susie and the lovely Julie". The girls were equally over dressed in sparkling dresses. "Ok this is how we do it. I will call the numbers and you will use the bingo dabbers supplied, stamp the number on your card if you have the number called. Any line vertical or horizontal is a winner, as are all the four corners, once a line has been won carry on with the same card to try for a full house which is every number on the card for a win".

"Ok my lovelies" and he stood with his hand on his hip doing the best I am little tea pot impression. "Downing Street Number Ten, box of tricks number six, garden gate number eight, and top of the shop number one". "House" a lady behind Liam shouted. "That was a quick call and what a pretty lady". The woman in her mid-thirties took her card to the front, she had covered all four corners. "Well done and what is your name and where are you from?" "My name is Michelle and I am from Masham in Yorkshire" "I would never have guessed with that accent Michelle!!" Everyone laughed. "Well you have just won yourself £300.00. A big hand for Michelle everyone". The night carried on in the same vein. With the compare playing the Larry Grayson card to the maximum. Liam and Jayne didn't win but both enjoyed the night. "Shall we call it a night Liam?" "Guess so" he said. They walked down the deck and Liam said goodnight. His room had been cleaned yet again, towels picked up where he had left them only a couple of hours earlier. The service is incredible he thought.

He was soon asleep and sure enough the dreams started again.

Mr Miller was cracking his bull whip, it was barely light but they made sure they got every ounce of work out of us. I was working with Lomo and every chance we got we talked but we had to be careful or Miller would throw a fit. I told Lomo I intended to escape and take Shona with me. "Are you stupid?" he asked "No, I am in love" "Well love will get you hung. You are a slave and you are branded on your buttock and you want to run away with a black girl. How do you think that will work?". Just then Miller came round the corner. "Did I hear you say black girl, boy?" "No Sir" "Well I best not hear a word out of you again or what will I do Cabhan?" "Whip me Sir" "Do you think I would be right to whip you boy?" I knew I had to say yes. "Yes I do Sir" "Then you best not let me catch you talking again". I kept my head down.

The rest of the day I was trying to figure out how I could escape with Shona. The night came, Lomo said that there was a meeting at the big house, Mr Grapes, Mr Miller and the overseers would be there until midnight so we could go to the laundry. I could hardly contain my excitement. As night fell Lomo beckoned me to follow him. Down we went into the basement, my beautiful Shona was waiting for me. We stayed for three hours and I told Shona of my plan. She said she was scared, if we got caught they would whip us and hang us from a tree.

"Shona I will protect you, we are going to get out of this and I will take you back to Ireland because this just ain't right" "Cabhan come on we have to go". Lomo went first, just as he opened the door a bright light shone at him lighting him up like a beacon. I scurried back down into the basement, I was shaking, I knew they had caught Lomo. I could hear the conversation. "Are you on your own boy?" "Yes Sir" "What were you doing in the laundry cellar?" "I was looking for food Sir" "So you were going to steal food hey boy?"

I knew if I had gone sooner we would have been safe but now poor Lomo was in it deep. Lomo was so frightened I heard them laughing. "Look the nigger pissed himself". Lomo was crying I couldn't do anything. "Tell you what I am going to do boy. I am going to sleep the drink off till the morning. I am going to tie you to the tree and I am going to whip your ass. Then nigger boy we are going to take you to see your fellow man on St Kitts, where they are playing the Master up, and there we will hang you from a tree so all you niggers get the message. Tie him to that tree boys and we will sort him in the morning".

"Do you want us to check the basement?" "No, they too stupid to share food he will have been on his own" and Grapes walked away. I went back and found Shona I told her what had happened and that I had to save Lomo, but one day I would be back for her. Shona cried and cried. "I won't forget about you Shona, I will be back for you" he promised. With that Cabhan grabbed a knife and sneaked out into the open grassy area, unsure of what he was going to do next, but he knew he had to save Lomo it was his best chance for redemption after what happened to Oday.

I could hear Lomo whimpering in the dark, so I followed the noise nobody was guarding him, so I cut him free. He hugged me. "Thank you my friend, but you know they will kill us both if they find us" "They won't find us. I am taking you home with me Lomo" "Where is home?" "Ireland my friend, Ireland".

I suddenly woke again at the same time 3.30am. What was the significance of this time? I showered and shaved and sat and watched the sun come up from the balcony. We were due to disembark for the next island at 10.00am. I met Jayne at 8.30am and we had a breakfast. The only word I can think of to describe the food was sumptuous. It was time to disembark for the island of Guadeloupe. They were met by guides and split into groups. Micah was Liam and Jayne's guide for the six hours that they would be on Guadeloupe. "Good morning ladies and gentlemen, my name is Micah I was born here on Guadeloupe. Most people don't know but we are actually two islands but a bridge was built so you can access both islands this way. The Italian Christopher Columbus was the first European to discover the island, although it is thought the Vikings in the 11th Century did come here, but did not have contact with the indigenous population of the time"

LOOKING FOR SHONA

"It was said Columbus was looking for fresh water when he stumbled upon what is now Guadeloupe, in November 1453. Our beautiful island has been under many different rulers, The British were here and the French, in fact the British gave the island to the French in order to keep Canada, which at the time they considered more important".

"Guadeloupe was a big sugar producer and with that came the horrors of slavery. Although some Masters did treat their slaves reasonably well, most did not and they were perceived as pieces of meat, to be used then sold on like animals". Liam could easily relate to this and he could see that his guide Micah was also quite upset by talking about it, so she probably came from slave stock too.

The small mini bus took them initially to the wooden bridge spanning the two islands.

"Ok everyone, you would at this point have to walk across the wooden bridge but because of time constraints we will stay

115

on this side as there are more things of interest for you. Our next stop is Carbet Falls. The falls attract over 400,000 visitors annually". They arrived at the Falls and were show vantage points to take pictures. "Stand there Liam, with the Falls in the background". Jayne produced her iPhone and snapped Liam smiling with the Falls complementing the picture in the background. Liam did the same for Jayne and then Jayne e-mailed the pictures to Jamie back at work. There was a quick reply back from Jamie. *"Lucky buggers LOL"*. "Seems like Jamie was impressed Liam" "Who wouldn't be hey Jayne?"

"Ok everyone, once you have all the pictures you need, we are heading over there to Jimbo's Creole Passion". Jimbo's was a white wooden building with an old tin roof the place seated about thirty people. Jimbo met everyone at the door and shook their hands. "I hope you will all like what I cook for you good people. I have prepared Fresh Shrimp Creole and Jambalaya, for you folks that have never had it. This dish is rice and chicken with Jimbo's special sauce. We also have our national dish Pork Columbo" "That's like a stew, I have had that Jayne" "Really, where?" "I honestly don't know, but I know I have had it".

"This guy is so entertaining Liam, he reminds of that Ainsley Harriott, who used to be on the telly all the time" "Yeah he is a bit of a cross between him and Lenny Henry, I agree" "This food is fabulous". They were at Jimbo's for almost an hour, the views were fabulous, it was red hot but with a slight breeze. "Ok everybody, I hope you have enjoyed the meal that Jimbo prepared for you". The party all clapped and Jimbo took a bow. "Right we are heading to our final destination before we head for the Cruise Liner".

"I think you will all enjoy this for sure. I have a few here that like a tipple, so we are heading for Damoiseau Distillery. Sorry about the state of the road, it's not something we tend to spend money on". Liam smiled, he turned to Jayne "You could hardly call it a road, it's more like a farmers track and dusty to boot" "It just adds to the ambience Liam, I love it, and I can't thank you enough. So glad I washed your clothes and made you meals when we shared at University" "Oh me too Jayne, or I would have been a mess back then" and he laughed. Once inside the quaint distillery, with its white painted walls and concrete floors, they were shown round the process and given a bit of history about why it was there. Jayne commented to Liam that the fumes alone were making her feel drunk.

Once again Liam felt an eerie feeling for the place, he seemed to know where to go and although he had never been in a distillery in his life, he seemed to understand the process. This is just weird he thought, but he didn't mention anything to Jayne for fear of ridicule, which he understood. He would think the same if he were not living this dual life.

After the tour and look around the shop, they made their way back to the ship. "Tonight's entertainment on board is Billy Boo, a comedian from Manchester. We have Play Your Cards Right and Strictly

Come Dancing. For guest's who would like to enter the Strictly competition, first prize is a holiday to Canada to see Niagara Falls followed by a week in New York, then you will be flown to Nashville home of the Grande Ole Oprey for four days before flying home. Everything is paid for and each couple will receive $4000 spending money". "Wow" the whole bus cried out. "You can dance Liam, shall we enter it?" "If you want Jayne, just a shame Jamie isn't here he loves dancing".

They arrived back at the ship. "Quick shower then Liam, and I'll meet you in the foyer say 8.30pm and will you put our names down for the Strictly Dancing thing?" "Will do Jayne, see you in a bit". Liam wandered over and signed his and Jayne's name into the competition, and then he headed to his room. He lay on the King sized bed still thinking about the distillery and wondering why he knew so much. There was a pattern to the dreams, he always returned to where the dream ended each time.

Liam showered and changed he had brought his tuxedo so dressed for the competition. He met Jayne, she was striking in a long blue evening dress with small gold flecks woven into the material. "I am guessing you two people are dressed for the competition? My name is Terry Ober and I will be with you and the other contestants during the competition. If you would like to follow me?" All the other contestants were already back stage. A total of eight couples had entered.

"Ok everybody please don't be nervous, I will be comparing tonight. We have four judges, Leslie Muller the ballerina, Dale Thorpe of Strictly Coming Dancing Fame, Debra Seaton actress and finally Maria Heath the TV Baker famous for Cakes are Special".

"So, ok let's do this". The big red curtains opened and the audience clapped Terry started introducing the couples, finally landing on Liam and Jayne. "So Liam and Jayne, you both look the part, are you married?" "No just good friends" "Both from the UK Liam?" "Yes, we are both from the UK".

"Ok our first couple up are Tracey Still and Alan Hilson, the first dance is a Rumba". Tracey and Alan were good and scored twenty four for the first dance. By the time it was Liam and Jayne's turn they were placed seventh, Alan and Tracey were leading. Jayne and Liam got a credible twenty three and the final couple Karen Bollinson and Nick Trill scored twenty five, which meant the three couples, went through to dance for the two places in the final. First up were Karen and Nick, dancing the quick step. "I think the judges were a bit harsh on Nick's timing Jayne, don't you?" "Well it is a big prize and they have to entertain the audience". Karen and Nick scored fourteen. "Next up, Jayne and Liam". Poor Liam got most of the steps wrong and they scored twelve. "What happened Liam?" "I don't know. I think the nerves got to me" It just left Tracey and Alan. "I fair hope they don't beat us Liam, that holiday would be fantastic". "Well, we have done well to get this far Jayne".

There was no stopping Tracey and Alan they scored twenty one then they went on to easily beat Karen and Nick in the final.

"Ladies and gentlemen, can we have a big round of applause for all the contestants and as a consolation prize for all of you, free drinks for the rest of the evening at the bar" "Well that's not bad Jayne" "Thought you might like that more than the holiday" and she laughed.

They retired to the bar with Liam making sure he had is fill for free. It was 12.10am when they retired to their respective rooms, Liam had quite a wobble on and Jayne helped him open his cabin door. He crashed on the bed and was soon back dreaming again.

Lomo was frightened. "Look Lomo, what choice do we have? They are going to whip you and hang you on St Kitts, I can't let that happen. Come on if we can get a rowing boat we will have six hours start on them". Nobody was watching the boats so Cabhan got a rowing boat with a sail, he then scuppered all the other boats hoping that this would slow them down even more. "Get in Lomo, grab an oar and paddle for all you are worth". Lomo nodded and off they set. By dawn they had made really good time. They didn't go to the first island, but landed at St Kitts for water and to see what food they could steal. They hid the boat in a small cove and covered it in branches.

They arrived in the town, which was just a ramshackle set of buildings. Cabhan was the one that stood out as everywhere he looked there were black people, which there would be, it was their island. Lomo blended in ok and they decided that it would be best if Cabhan hid while Lomo tried to find food and water for their journey. He had been gone almost three hours, when from a distance Cabhan could hear a commotion going on. A well-dressed white man was shouting, something about, 'we either cut his hands off or we string him up or shall I do both?'

There were two other big white men aside the well-dressed man. I suddenly realised it was my friend Lomo, he had been caught. There was nothing I could do, I watched as first the big white man cut off Lomo's left hand then his right hand and he was bleeding and screaming. "Now string the thief up boys". I could feel tears rolling down my cheeks, one day I thought, I will avenge my friend. Poor Lomo had passed out so the hanging wasn't bad for him. I waited all day and went over and cut Lomo down. It was then that I inscribed the date and his name on a stone at the base of the tree for him to be remembered by. I could do no more for my friend so I headed back to the boat, luckily for me I passed a house and managed to steal water and something resembling fruit cake and a couple of melons. I waited until dusk then set off again the wind was good and I made good time. I was in the open Ocean and felt quite scared, when in the distance I could see a large ship. Not knowing who or what it was I was feeling nervous. If it was unfriendly they would take me back to my certain death.

The huge ship turned out to be the 'Annabelle'; she was King Charles' 1st ship under the stewardship of Captain Russell. They were very kind to me, I told them my story and Captain Russell, who was a 'God fearing' man, told me they were on their way back from the Caribbean. He said he did not agree with the slavery of white men, so he would let me stay on board and would drop me off on the West Coast of Ireland, where he would give me some food and water and a small boat, but I would have to row for about four days to the coast. I thanked him and said I would work for my passage, which the kindly man accepted graciously. The men were basically nice, one or two would call me names. But on the whole the journey was good. They put me in a boat with food and water and I rowed solid for four days before landing at a small deserted beach that I believed to be Ballydrew.

Home at last. Two boys about thirteen were fishing in the rock pools. "How are ye lads?" "Where you come from Mister?" came the reply. "Oh, just been out fishing. You can have the boat lads if you can tell me where I am". The boys looked all puzzled "Ye at Ballydrew of course" they chirped. "This is Claire Island and Claw Bay is five miles that way" and he pointed his grubby little hand north. "Well thank ye boys, good luck with the fishing".

I thought I recognised the area but having left at fourteen and with everything that had gone on in my life it was taking some remembering. On the road to Claw Bay I saw somebody I thought I knew walking towards me, she was dressed in all black. "Mary Connelly as I live and breathe", Mary looked at me. "It's me Cabhan!!" "Bloody hell, we thought you was dead lad" "I nearly bloody was Mary" "Where you been?" she asked. "If I told you, it would be hard for you to believe Mary" "I lost my Dermot to that bloody war so times have been tough Cabhan" "I wondered why all the black clothes" "Well ye know its tradition lad, when thee loses a loved one". "How's me mammy Mary?" "Sorry Cabhan, she passed two years back. Your sister still lives in Claw Bay, she done well for herself, she married an older man remember Mr

Sumpt?" "Old Sumpty? Where we used to go scroggin for apples?" "Yeah that's him, well he owns half of County Mayo and he married your sister and they say he's not long to live. They have no children so the fortune passes onto Kate. Sure you will be all-right there lad?" Cabhan felt speechless, his sister Kate was a beauty, she was five years older than Cabhan but he could remember all the lads from Claw Bay and the surrounding villagers wanted Kate's hand. "I best keep walking Mary, will see you around" "Sure you will" "See you soon Mary" "I'll be looking forward to that too be sure". Cabhan carried on his journey.

Without fail 3.30am was the time when Liam woke out of his sleep. He now knew why he felt sick on St Kitts when he had seen the stone with the writing on, it was for his friend Lomo. Liam sat pondering. Two glasses of whisky later and he was asleep again. He didn't dream anymore but was woken by a loud banging on the door. "Liam, Liam" Jayne was at the door. "Hurry up we are here?" "Where?" he asked "Lucia, as they say or St Lucia as we would say" "Blimey Jayne. Sorry woke up at 3.30pm and fell back to sleep, I will be with you in a minute". "I will wait in the queue in the lobby, but hurry up". Liam arrived a bit flustered. "Sorry Jayne" "This is the last island before we go to Barbados isn't it Liam?" "Yeah we should hire a Jeep or something to see Barbados" "That sounds like a good idea Liam".

They were met at the quay side by one of the guides. "Ok looks like you are the last in this party". Jayne looked at Liam smiled and shook her head. "Ok well my name is Judy and I am your guide for the time you are on this island. We only have three hours here I am afraid, so my suggestion would be to find a nice bar have a meal and relax. The coach will pick you up at 5.00pm sharp, please don't be late" and the guide shot her eyes at Jayne and Liam. "That sounds good to me, after all the rushing about we have done Liam" "Agreed Jayne, lets go slightly off the beaten track and find a bar". They walked for twenty minutes across a warm white sandy beach, eventually finding a small bar with a jetty.

"This looks like the place what a great name" "I didn't notice, what did it say Jayne?" "It said Jankay and Oday's place, 'meat to please you, pleased to meet you'" Across the door it said 'Arrive a stranger, leave a friend". Liam went cold what is this all about. He couldn't tell Jayne so he just played along with it. "Hi folks" came the friendly voice. "My name is Jack Rice and where are you good people from?" "Both from the UK" said Jayne. "I am guessing you are from Scotland?" "Yes my family moved here in 1981 and I bought this bar in 1997. You are sitting in a very famous bar". Liam saw his chance. "Noticed the name, what is the significance?" "Well legend has it that Oday was a mute and was whipped and then hung for running away from Barbados. His friend was Jankay, he was sold for running away and I believe another slave, who may have been white, was punished but I don't know where or how".

Liam had to be careful not to raise suspicions with Jayne so he started to ask about the bar hoping more of the story would unfold. "Let me get your drinks and I will tell you the story" "What are you having?" "Shall we have two Oday's please?" "What's in them, Jack?" "Rum, ginger ale, vodka, grenadine and gin then loaded with pineapple, strawberry and mango. Do you require food also?" "Just a couple of your Cheese Toasties please Jack" "My chef will sort for you. Now back to the story" Jack started to tell a story about two slaves but it didn't match what Liam already knew so he felt a bit disappointed but didn't show it.

It was 4.15pm before they knew it so they thanked Jack for an entertaining afternoon and they headed to the pickup point for the coach. Liam was feeling a bit confused about his friends and the story that Jack had told them. I guess stories get altered he thought. So much on this trip was making sense and verifying his dreams he just wished he could share the experience. As usual they were the last ones on the coach on the trip back to the boat. The guide said she had everyone's name in a hat and the first six couples out would sit at the Captains table if they so wished. She proceeded to ask different people to pull names out. "Mr and Mrs Neal, John and Becky Saunders, Miss Tracey Still and Alan Hilson, Miss Jayne Tupton and Mr Liam Egan, Susan Bolly and Mary Duke and finally one more lucky couple, Donna Goldfield and Androv Miklenko. You are invited to be the guest of the captain tonight at the top table. We also have a group from the seventies called Showaddy Waddy and a great comedian from the same era, Kenny Plunkett. Ok everyone, I hope you enjoyed your visit to St Lucia, we will sail tonight for Barbados which is our final destination. Have a lovely time tonight and if I am not your chosen guide for Barbados, have a safe journey thank you".

"We have to be at the Captains table for 8pm Liam, so don't fall asleep. I will meet you in the Foyer at 7.45pm" "Ok promise I will be there" he said and they parted to go to their rooms. Liam really wanted to sleep to catch up on his dreams but knew he had to be down for the evening meal because Jayne was so excited.

After showering and changing they met in the Foyer and were shown to their seats. Jayne was next to the Captain, as was Tracey Still, then Liam and next to Jayne was Alan, Tracey's partner. The Captain proposed a toast "My crew and I hope you have had an excellent Caribbean cruise we will arrive at our final destination and you will then stay two nights at the Royal Carumba Hotel for two nights. There you will receive an opulent service at a fabulous five star hotel before flying home. So I would like to thank my crew, who I am sure have been attentive at all times and have made your holiday one you will remember forever. The crew" and he raised his glass of champagne.

Next up a gentleman in a dinner suit, with long coat tails, announced the first course. "Ladies and gentlemen, for your pleasure tonight's first course is Walnut, Aragula and Gorgonzola Crostini please enjoy". Liam soon tucked in to his food. Jayne was speaking with the Captain. Tracey asked Liam what he did for a living. "I am a trader in the Stock Exchange in London" "What does your girlfriend do?" "Oh Jayne isn't my girlfriend, we are just mates, we've known each other since our University days". "Sorry, I wasn't prying" "No that's ok. What about you?" "Well Alan is the same to me as Jayne is to you, he does my books and we have been friends for years" "What books are those?" "My accounts, I have stables in Derbyshire. I school horses and have about twenty stables".

"Ladies and gentlemen, your second course is being served. Fresh shrimp on ice, with a Caribbean sauce" "I'm filling up already Liam, don't know about you" "I know what you mean Tracey. Have you always had horses?" "Well I've always ridden but stopped horse riding from about twenty until I was twenty six" "Why was that?" "I went travelling. You know the student thing, Australia, New Zealand Thailand and all that" "Sounds great" "Yes I enjoyed it and then one day I thought it was time to grow up. So I came home got a bank loan and set up my business and never I've looked back".

With the second course done the speaker informed them of course three. Aragula salad with mushroom stuffed salmon lox balls. "So are you looking forward to Barbados?" Liam could not tell how much this was the one part he had been waiting for. "Yes, I'm looking forward to Barbados Tracey".

The course and palate cleansers kept coming. The last course to arrive was Montreal Peppered steak, on a bed of sea weed, with baby carrots and cracked wine roast potatoes. Hardly anybody had the dessert that followed afterwards, but Jayne noticed the Captain finished everything. Must be used to it she thought.

The dancing started. "Come on Liam I love this". Showaddy Waddy introduced themselves to one of their big hits "Let's go for a little walk under the moon of love" Liam was twirling Jayne about, very nearly knocking Tracey and Alan over.

"Whoops sorry you two" "No problem Liam, you go for it" "I think she's got the hot's for you Silver Tongue!!" "Behave yourself, Tupton" joked Liam.

Four dances later, Liam went to the bar for a drink for him and Jayne. "Well fancy seeing you here" "Sorry Tracey didn't see you there. Would you and Alan like a drink?" "Alan has gone to bed, he said he felt ill. A bloody elephant would have felt ill with the amount of food he devoured, Liam" and she laughed. "Well come and join me and Jayne if you want" "Sure you don't mind?" "Of course not, told you me and Jayne are just mates" "Hi Jayne, I didn't get chance to really introduce myself, Tracey Still" "Nice to meet you Tracey" "Hope you don't mind, I met Liam at the bar and my friend has gone off to bed, so he said I could join you two". Jayne didn't mind she didn't have feelings in that way for Liam, but they were best mates and she wanted to enjoy the holiday with him.

The night ended on a bit of a low for Jayne, she felt like a gooseberry while

Tracey and Liam sat talking. Out of the blue Tracey said "I will leave you two to it, I need my beauty sleep, probably see you around tomorrow on Barbados" and she left. "Your charm not working, Egan?" "Ha Ha very funny Tupton, think I will call it a night. Looking forward to Barbados, are you Jayne?" "Yeah, it's one of those places I have always wanted to go to" "Ok, well I'll see you about 9.00am in the foyer tomorrow". They both went off to their cabins.

Once inside, Liam opened a bottle of lager out of the fridge and lay on the bed. He was soon fast asleep and back in his other world. His dream carried on where it had finished last time, with Cabhan waving goodbye to Mary and walking the four miles to Claw Bay. 'There was nowhere in the world as pretty as Claw Bay' they used to say. The path to Claw Bay hugged the cliff tops like a new born babe to its mother. Cabhan carried on down the dirt track until he eventually came to Tree Cliff Hall. A massive, dark foreboding place, that nestled on the top of the cliffs overlooking Claw Bay. He walked towards the tree lined drive and could see through the big Iron gates there was a circular piece in front of the house with a big water fountain with a bronze horse spewing water out of its mouth. In front of the Grand oak doors was a black buggy, he could see his sister just getting out of it. He shouted "Kate, Kate" Kate looked up and realising it was her little brother she ran to him. "Cabhan" and she threw her arms round him. "Where have you been?" "All in good time Kate. Could I have some food and a drink?" "Of course you must stay with me and my husband" "I heard Mammy had passed on" he said. "Yes, she was heartbroken when you left Cabhan" "I also hear you married old Darrin Sumpt". Mary put her finger to her lips to tell Cabhan to be quiet. She then whispered in his ear. "Look Cabhan, Darrin is very old but he was good to me and Mammy and this life I have now, I could only have dreamt of, so please show him respect" "Sorry Sis, I will".

"Cabhan, Darrin has only day's to live, he doesn't want to see anyone only his nurse and me" "Oh I am so sorry Kate". "Darrin is a lot older than me and it was a marriage of convenience for both of us. I love him but not in that way" "Is it true you are his only beneficiary Sis?" "I believe so. Now tell me Cabhan, where did you go?" "I was taken by pirates to the Caribbean, they said we were going to be indentured servants but that's some fancy word for slavery. Sis, I have done some bad things to survive". "What do you mean?" "I killed a man who was going to whip me, he said I had stolen an apple, but I hadn't. The Master said I could have one. I could not stand being beaten again it's so degrading and really hurts Sis. I buried this man's body and I ran to the beach where my two friends were mending boats. Their names were Oday and Jankay. They were Negro slaves. Without going into the full story, Oday would have been alive today if they hadn't helped me. Jankay was sold as a slave and one day I will go back and buy his freedom Sis. I met a girl also, a black girl, her name is Shona. They made us make a baby Sis, but the baby died and time passed. I didn't know what happened to Shona. Then I ended working in the

furniture shop and made friends with a
negro called Lomo, he found Shona and
we started meeting. Then Lomo was
caught, they did terrible things to him Sis,
too bad to tell you. I told Shona I was
going to escape but that I would come
back for her and I will" "Sounds like ye
love that lass, Cabhan" "I do that very
much Sis".

Kate called over a girl servant, "Make a
bed up for my brother in the West Wing
please Bridie" "Yes ma'am" she said.
"Blimey, that is really weird, them calling
ye Ma'am" "You get used to it" "I hope
ye treats em well Sis?" "Of course I do I
have been a servant myself, don't forget".

"So how come you ended up here?" "Well
Mum worked in the kitchen and I used to
come up here and sit outside and wait for
her. One day Mam said the Master wanted
to see me. He sat me and Mammy down
and said he wanted my hand in marriage
and that me and Mammy would never
want for anything ever again. He has
never touched me Cabhan he is a
gentleman really is" "Then why did he

want thee?" "He said he didn't want to be lonely anymore. I went to England, to London, you should see that place. Darrin knew everyone even the King" "Look Sis, can we talk tomorrow? I am knackered". "Of course, silly me" said Kate, "Bridie show Mr Cabhan to his room. I will see you in the morning Cabhan". Cabhan leaned forward and kissed Kate. "Love you Sis". Kate had a tear rolling down her pretty white porcelain face. The feeling that her brother was still alive and was back in her life gave her a feeling of euphoria. Kate had prayed, many times, that one day her little brother would come back and now he had, she sure wasn't going to let him out of her sight.

The following morning Kate took Cabhan into town for clothes. Timmid was the nearest town to Claw Bay, about fourteen miles by buggy. Kate picked out ten suits with shirts and shoes to match. "You are so handsome my little brother and every inch the country gentleman" "How will I ever be able to pay you back Sis?" "You don't have to pay me back; payment is having you back in my life".

"We need to give you a purpose now Cabhan and a wage, will you be the Estate Manager for Tree Cliff Hall?" "What and I will get a wage?" "You will get a handsome wage Cabhan and if you are frugal, you will be able to save money and free your Shona and your friend Jankay" "Kate you don't know how much I am in your debt for this".

They headed back from Timmid the roads were very uneven so they were bounced up and down and side to side during their journey back to Tree Cliff Hall. As soon as the buggy stopped, two footmen came out and helped Kate and Cabhan out of the buggy. "Take the luggage and put it in Mr Cabhan's room please". The two footmen did as they were asked. "Go to the drawing room Cabhan, while I check on Darrin". Kate had been gone a few minutes when Cabhan heard a horrific scream. He ran out of the drawing room and met Kate on the Grand hall staircase. "Kate what is it? What is a matter?" "Darrin is dead Cabhan, he died while we were in town" she sobbed. Cabhan really did not know what to say, so he just held his sister and comforted her. "Get me a large brandy" he said to one of the servants. "Here Kate, drink this, it will help with the shock". The biggest shock was yet to come. For days Kate cried after the funeral she heard from Darrin's solicitor.

"Dear Mrs Sumpt,

Greetings and Salutations.

I hope my letter finds you in good health, although in somewhat sad times. The reading of Mr Sumpt's last will and testament shall be at my offices. Number 23, Cades Avenue, Knightsbridge at 2.30pm on Wednesday 23rd June. Your attendance would be much appreciated.

My very best wishes,
God speed and a safe journey.

Yours truly
Mister William Money.

Because the will reading was to be in London, Kate asked Cabhan to accompany her. "Of course I will Kate" "We will need to leave Ireland on Friday, to ensure we arrive at the Solicitors office on time Cabhan" "I shall have the horses ready for the buggy".

Liam woke with a start, at the almost annoying time of 3.30am. 'What the hell was the significance of this time?' It was if he was reading a book, then at exactly 3.30am the lights would go out and he was left wondering what happened.

Liam got up and checked his emails on his tablet. There was one from Jamie just telling him that he had won the works golf tournament and that he was now top dog for the year. Liam had won it three years on the trot but had forgotten about it when he booked the cruise, much to Jamie's delight as he had the bragging rights now. Jamie went on to ask if he was ok, as he and Millie were concerned for him. Typically Jamie, Liam thought, total competitor but a big softie at heart. Liam nodded off again but no dreams came to

LOOKING FOR SHONA

him. He showered and shaved and headed down to meet Jayne. He felt excited about Barbados, but also a little apprehensive, being here could give him so many answers but also maybe more intrigue.

Jayne was ready for Barbados, dressed in her shorts and blouse with wide brimmed hat. "Quite the aficionado, Miss Tupton, I very much the Audrey Hepburn look" "Ha, ha, I wish Liam"

"Ok everybody my name is Sissy, I am here to help you to see and enjoy our beautiful island. You will see all the Vendors with their trips to various parts of this island. We have lots to see and do. I would recommend you do at least one of the trips to the Plantations, to hear about our history and how the island was colonised. Any questions, please don't hesitate to ask".

"Jayne, I really want to see a Plantation". Liam knew which one, if only he could find it. "I'm easy Liam, whatever you want to do. Look there is a trip there to the Latte Plantation, shall we go on that?"

"Let's just have a look first". Each vendor showed a picture of the master's house, so Liam was hoping his would be there. He walked up and down the line but could not see it. Jayne at this point was getting tired. "Just pick one Liam, they will all be the same". "Maybe to you" he thought "but not for me".

Then, just as he was about to give up he knew the house. It was called Marion House. He didn't know if that was its name when he was there in his dreams, but he knew the house, it was embedded in his mind. "Let's go for this one" "Are you sure Liam? Everyone seems to be going for the Latte Plantation" "I think this one looks more authentic". Liam paid, and along with two other couples, they were taken out into the country, Marion House was close to the shore line. Things were flooding back. The man taking them didn't speak much, but they were met by a black girl. She said her name was Mulie. Mulie was olive skinned and quite tall. "Hi my name is Mulie and I am a direct descendant of a slave, who lived and worked this Plantation. Although my grandfather, many times over, lived here in 1627, he was sold and then lived on St Lucia. He was bought again, but all trace of him on that day ceased, so I don't know if he died on the island, but as was tradition they made the strongest slaves bare a child with a white woman. My great grandma was Irish, but she lived her days out in St Lucia, as did all my descendants".

Liam asked if she knew the name of the slave that was her many times removed grandparent. "Yes his name was Jankay. In fact he had a bar named after him on St Lucia" "Hey that's where we went Liam, is this the bar that Jack Rice owns" she asked. Mulie said, "That's correct" "But he tells a different story to yours" "To be honest, Jack makes the stories up for the holiday makers, we all laugh about it but mine is the true story". Liam felt elated it was all starting to fit together. Jankay must have got off the island, he wondered if he had moved to another island or if he had found freedom.

"If you would all like to follow me, this is the area where the slaves lived, in a hut similar to these. These are not the original huts, they went many years ago, but they have been created from drawings found in the house. If you were black and strong didn't matter if you were man or woman, you cut sugar cane from dawn to dusk and you would be in team one. If you were not so strong, or you had been ill, you went into team two. You still had to work, but it wasn't as hard. The same family owned this property until 1963, when it was purchased by the government as a place of interest, so it is now protected".

"Who were the owners?" "The family name was, Slaley Morton. In fact Humphrey Slaley Morton's son was made a Sir, for his services to the realm". Liam could hardly hide his excitement. "Sorry to keep asking questions but the bar on St Lucia was called Oday and Jankay's bar, I think? Who was Oday?" "I'm sorry, I know very little. All we know is he was Jankay's best friend, but I don't know any more than that". Liam wanted to share his story but knew that wasn't possible.

"Right we'd best move on. This is the garden where the vegetables and fruit were grown for the big house. Slaves worked here but if they were ever caught stealing they would be severely punished and maybe even hung, depending on how the Overseer was feeling that day. Legend has it that an Overseer was murdered in this very spot by a slave who had pinched an apple". Liam wanted to put the story straight but knew he couldn't. How history weaves its many indiscretions then rewrites them.

"Below here is the basement. These were the laundry rooms of the day and also where the clothes were mended. It would have been very misty down here with all the steam coming off the clothes. There would have been about twelve girls down here and they would live, eat and sleep down here. Quite often these girls were hand-picked by the Master who would, to put it mildly, entertain these girls at his will".

"Ok follow me. We will now go into the furniture workshop. Mainly white boys, but some Negroes would work here, as indentured apprentices. Their term would be seven years, then after that they became craftsmen and would quite often be released as free men. Many chose to stay and worked for the Master, but as free men, the conditions were not too bad, but their Masters were very strict and they were made to work hard and not allowed to make mistake or they would be whipped mercilessly". One of the couple turned to Liam and said "We could do with that in the UK now, then the youngsters would show some respect". Liam had all on not to punch his lights out. 'Stupid man' he thought, 'if only you knew'.

"Ok everyone, feel free to look round. Our next stop will be the house. Surprisingly many artefacts from the house still remain, some going back to the original Humphrey Slaley Morton's days". After the three couples had finished wandering the workshop they climbed the wooden stairs on to the wrap round veranda and then in through the main entrance. The opulence of the building was there for all

149

to see. "You are free to wander; I would ask you don't cross the red ropes or touch anything please. Feel free to ask any question". They wandered about the house but Liam didn't notice anything special, but then he wasn't allowed in the house much.

"Ok everybody, before we head back to the port for lunch, we have just a couple of things to show you. If you are squeamish or don't like things associated with death. Then please go and sit on the coach. The ladies of the house would sit on the porch for afternoon tea in the baking hot sunshine. Can you imagine being a slave, watching them eating and drinking when you were thirsty and hungry? This tree, here, was the tree used to punish any slave, man or woman, that stepped out of line. They would be bound by their hands and arms, stripped naked, then whipped. When they passed out through the sheer pain, they would then be hung by the neck from this very branch".

Suddenly Liam was sick. "You ok Liam?" "Very sorry folks, I must have picked up a tummy bug "You sure you are ok Sir?" "Yes, I will be fine honestly". There's just one last thing to see. This is a gravestone of riddles, nobody knows who is buried here or if in fact if anyone is buried here. If you look closely there is a poem and two names on the stone which are barely visible. The first name you can make out a letter N and a letter Y but nothing else and the second name you can detect a letter H and a letter N. The poem is a bit clearer; I will read it out to you. Where the words have almost disappeared I have put in the words I think have eroded.

FRIENDS

If ye could take a minute
to help ye understand
I am a better person
because ye are my friend.

It really doesn't matter
if we're together or apart
for I swept you up into my hands
and placed you in my heart.

And ye at any moment

151

LOOKING FOR SHONA

ye ever start to doubt
there's a special bond between us
that we shall not live without.

Ye truly are the answers
to many of me prayers
I need someone to stand beside me
to help comfort and to cope
to remind me that there's always
some room for one to hope.

You've helped me through all those
things
that only ye could do
I never knew what friendship was
until I first met ye.

And if I had one simple wish
it would surely be
that God would keep ye in my life
throughout all eternity.

And now I hope ye realise
just how much you mean to me.
Ye are the definition
of what a real, true friend should be.

Your True Friend

It didn't seem to mean much to Liam so he shrugged it off. He felt emotional as it was just some random stone in the ground with a poem on it. It really wasn't that big a deal, not when he had been in the garden, where he killed and buried a man. He had seen the laundry, which was the last place he had seen Shona, and the tree where poor Oday was whipped within an inch of his life and then hung like a dog to die.

"If you would all like to get back on the coach, we will be calling at the capital of Barbados, which is Bridgetown, where we have arranged lunch at Fishy Waves, possibly the best fish restaurant in the Caribbean".

After the meal they had free time to shop. Jayne bought a small gold ring she said it would remind her forever of the great time they had on the Cruise. Liam felt a bit selfish knowing the real reason he had come here, was to substantiate his dreams, and it had.

On the way back to the hotel the guide said the hotel had a karaoke from 8.00pm until 10.00pm, then a disco from 10.00pm until 2.00am. Evening meal would be served from 6.00pm until 8.30pm. Jayne and Liam agreed to meet at 7.30pm at the restaurant. "I'm going to have five minutes Liam, it's been a long, but most enjoyable day don't you think?" "Great Jayne, I love this place". His words really hid the truth, that it held only bad memories for him and Cabhan. Liam shaved and showered then sat on the patio with a bottle of beer trying to unravel the things he had seen and heard about today.

Liam made his way to the foyer to meet Jayne, he was spot on time much to Jayne's surprise. "Blimey Egan, what's up with you, on time that's a first?" "Behave Tupton or I will make you dance to the birdy song" "My lips are now sealed Liam" and they both laughed.

LOOKING FOR SHONA

There were three restaurants in the hotel, an Italian, a Chinese and Spanish. They decided on the Italian restaurant for their meal. Liam had just a main course which was the Bella Lasagne and Jayne opted for the Alfredo Carbonara. They both opted for the Tiramisu to finish.

"Did you enjoy yours Jayne?" he asked. "It was ok nothing to write home about" she said, "What about you?" "Mine was the same, although the Tiramisu was good, but then the Italians really know how to make that dessert".

"So what's the plan?" "Well, I am going to have a go on the Karaoke, do you fancy singing something with me Jayne?" "Oh no! I will let you play the fool tonight Mr Egan" "Ha, ha nice words Tupton".

Liam was soon strutting his stuff. First he sang 'The Gambler' by Kenny Rogers then he did 'Carol' by Neil Sedaka. He was just about to leave the stage when he spotted Tracey Still. "Hey Tracey, get up here and do a Sonny and Cher number with me". Tracey just smiled, but Liam wasn't giving up. "Come on he cajoled. Eventually Tracey succumbed to Liam's pestering. They nailed the song "I Got You Babe" Everyone clapped and they took a bow. "Where are you sitting Tracey?" "Near the back, we were a bit late coming down. I am afraid Alan told me he wanted more than just a friendship. He was really quite upset, I really don't know what to do and I could see he was mad when you were calling me to sing with you, so I best go and sit with him" "Understand, let's make sure we get each other's phone numbers before we leave tomorrow" "Will do Liam". Tracey walked back to the back of the room and Liam sat back down with Jayne. "Blown out again Egan?" "You reckon Tupton? Time will tell" he said.

The Karaoke came to a close and the disco started. Liam by this time was quite merry. Jayne had been pacing herself whilst on the other hand Liam had been hammering the sherbets. Now ignoring what Tracey had told him earlier he wandered over to where Tracey and Alan were sat. "Hey Alan, do you mind if I take the pretty lady for a dance?" Alan glared at Liam "Why should I mind?". With that Tracey was straight up and they danced first to The Three Degrees classic 'When will I see you again', then Chris De Burgh's 'Lady in Red'. At the end of the song Tracey whispered in Liam's ear. "I best sit down, I don't want to ruin the holiday for Alan. I will slip my mobile number under your door, call me when you get back in the UK". Tracey left Liam on the dance floor and headed back to a slightly miffed Alan at the back of the room.

The problem with Liam was that he tended to get very loud when he was drunk, so by the time midnight came a couple of the waiters had to escort him back to his room. He wasn't an aggressive drunk, just a loud drunk. They opened the room door for Liam. "Would you like a drink with me gentlemen?" Liam said, in a just coherent voice. "Maybe another time,

Sir. Sleep well goodnight" and they closed the door to Liam's room.

Liam fell over taking his shoes off and then crashed onto the bed and fell sound asleep.

The dream started again. Cabhan and Kate's journey started towards London, it would be an arduous journey. They finally arrived at a boarding house close to where the offices of William Money were located.

They paid the landlady for the room. She said they had to share as she was full, because King Charles was going to be riding through London tomorrow from his retreat up North as she put it. The room was dimly lit there were two beds, a settee that had seen better days and a polished wooden floor. In the corner was a bowl with a large jug of water. "Shall we go out into London Sis?" "Not sure Cabhan, they say there are people who will rob you" "They are very welcome to try Sis".

LOOKING FOR SHONA

They walked the streets of London, passing by people sat on steps drinking Gin and slobbering over each other. "How dreadful is this place Cabhan?" "Oh we will be ok; we only have to stop until tomorrow, once the will is read we are out of here".

Eventually Cabhan found an Ale house, it wasn't the best, but wasn't has bad as some they had looked in. After an hour a man came over to their table. This man was about six feet three with straggly black hair, he had clothes similar to those of a buccaneer. When he opened his mouth, most of his teeth were rotten and he smelt like a wild hog.

"My name is PJ Mawgan. I have been watching you and I believe I may know you Sir". Cabhan could feel the panic travel from his head to his boots. "I have to say, the last time I saw you, your clothes did not have the look of finery such as they do now Sir. I believe your name is Cabhan, am I correct Sir?" Kate immediately spoke seeing that Cabhan had frozen. "I don't know what you want

LOOKING FOR SHONA

Mister, but me and my husband are just about to leave. Come on Sean; let us leave this fool to his thoughts". Cabhan rose to get up. "Did you call me a fool sweet lady?" "Look we don't want any trouble mister" said Cabhan. "You sit down slave boy; I will deal with you in a minute. Mr Grapes is going to be so pleased I have found you".

Cabhan knew the game was up as two more of Mawgan men came and stood by his side. He knew he had one chance, he picked up the chair and hit all three men across the side of the face. They dropped like a stack of dominoes that had been pushed over. "Run Sis" Cabhan shouted. For good measure Cabhan kicked all three men while they were down and left them groaning on the floor. They ducked down the small alley ways running for all they were worth. After about a mile they stopped and looked back there was nobody in pursuit. They then walked back to the boarding house. "Oh Cabhan, I can't begin to think what my little brother has been through. I am so pleased we are together again" "Sis it was hell, no person

160

should have to endure that in their life". They both managed to get some sleep. The following morning they arrived at William Money's offices for the will reading.

The offices were quite grand. William Money was a tall thin man, dressed all in black with a white shirt and black tie. "Welcome Mrs Sumpt and you are?" Sumpt asked as he turned to look at Cabhan. "He is my brother Mr Sumpt, he has chaperoned me from Ireland because it is such a long journey for a mere woman to take on her own" "I understand Mrs Sumpt".

"Well, let us begin with the will" Said Mr Money.

"I Darrin Sumpt on this day of June 17th in the year of our lord 1632, do declare this to be my final will and testament before god and my witness.

Mr Sumpt's witness was a close confidante of King Charles 1ˢᵗ, a Mr Thomas Wentworth".

"Mr Sumpt owned land in County Mayo, totalling some two thousand leagues, he also owned land in Suffolk England totalling a further three thousand leagues. All land he leaves to his wife Kate. Tree Cliff Hall, Claw Bay in McConlough, County Mayo, along with the fifty eight properties across Ireland he also leaves to Kate. His four houses in England, three in the County of Suffolk and one in the city of London, he leaves to Kate Sumpt, his lawful wife. All monies, totalling £440,000, he also leaves to Kate.

A small orchard, in McConlough, he leaves to Thomas Wentworth his witness and signatory on the will".

"That concludes the reading of the will, do you have any questions Mrs Sumpt? I have prepared the documents, if you will sign them and you Sir, witness the signature then all the afore mentioned will be signed over to you Mrs Sumpt". Kate signed the documents with Cabhan. She felt quite uneasy and looked shocked at her husband's wealth, this had been a poor girl from Claw Bay who possibly was now one of the wealthiest women in Ireland. She thanked Mr Money. Cabhan and Kate left for the boat back to Ireland.

Kate was very quiet on the way back to Claw Bay. "Are you ok Sis?" "I knew Darrin was quite rich, but I never expected this fortune Cabhan". "Well, all I can say is lucky you, Sis" "I know Cabhan, I am so lucky to have you back home to help and share in my good fortune. We now have the burial of Darrin to sort". It was 3.00am in the morning, four days later, when the buggy carrying Cabhan and Kate pulled up in front of the big oak doors at Tree Cliff House.

It was 3.30am again, when Liam woke from his dream. There were still drunken revellers playing in the pool, directly below his balcony. Liam got up for a glass of water, his head felt it was going to explode and his mouth was so dry it felt like the bottom of a bird cage. He wandered over to the window with his glass of water and to his amazement he could see Jayne in the pool. She looked like she was having a great time. Liam thought about shouting to her but then thought it might be construed wrong, so he wandered back to bed.

There were no more dreams and with his case packed, he decided to wander down to Jayne's room to check if she was ok. As he left the room he noticed a piece of folded paper, it was Tracey's mobile number, she had written her number and underneath she put "Lovely to meet you, call me and hopefully we can see each other again, Tracey xx". He put the note in his wallet, thinking to himself, wait until I tell Miss Tupton after she said I had "lost it", indeed. And he smiled to himself. He knocked on Jayne's door to see if she was ready. After a few seconds Jayne appeared looking more like Medusa than Jayne. Her hair was every where, her make-up had run she just looked generally dreadful. "What time is it Liam?" she asked groggily. "8.45 am, we are leaving at 10.00pm. I thought we could have a coffee and maybe a croissant". The thought of food had Jayne running to the toilet to be sick. "Shall I take that as a 'no' then?" "You go Liam, I need to sort myself out, I will be there at ten" "Ok see you on the coach".

Tracey's coach was leaving at 9.00 am and as Liam entered the foyer she was about to get on the coach, she waved and blew a kiss. Liam felt quite pleased with himself, maybe this is what he needed to get the dreams and Shona out of his life.

After a coffee and a croissant Liam got on the coach, and sat halfway up so that he could check Jayne was on her way. The rep got on and started doing a head count. "One missing. Is it your wife Mr Egan?" "Well actually Jayne is my friend, not my wife and she is about to get on the coach now". Liam was thinking 'stick that where the sun doesn't shine you cow'. Jayne sat next to Liam and hardly spoke, she was soon asleep for the journey to the plane,

Almost at the airport Liam's phone vibrated in his pocket. When he looked at the screen he was shocked it was a message from Joan. He opened the message it said, "Liam I am sorry I have not been in touch, it isn't that I don't like you in fact quite the opposite but it's complicated and you would struggle to understand. I will be in touch" 'How odd' Liam thought. By now they were about to go into the airport. "Come on Jayne, we are at the airport". Jayne wiped her mouth. "Oh Liam, I feel so crap, never again". "You only live once girl". The Captain announced the flight would be eight hours and twenty seven minutes into Heathrow, London.

Liam settled down watched a couple of films, read the flight magazine and the whole time Jayne slept, missing her food, although Liam did think that wasn't such a bad thing.

Eventually they landed at Heathrow. Jayne was a bit better, although not her one hundred percent best. Once through customs, Liam called a taxi, dropping Jayne off first and then him.

Back in his apartment, Liam sat on his settee looking out over the Thames and was thinking about all he had heard from the rep on Barbados and the other things on the islands. He also thought, why after all this time, did Joan get in touch and why the mystery?

Once back at work the usual banter evolved questions like, were him and Jayne an item now? all the usual boy bravado stuff. Millie called Jamie to say she had made Liam his favourite Bubble and Squeak potato cakes with British Bangers and Asparagus in batter with dipped cheese. "You can't refuse that mate at ours" "You are bang on there, Jamie it's my favourite" "You would think you and Millie were married the way she likes to cook for you" "Let the best man win I say" "You have no chance Egan, your ex-girlfriends talk" and he put up his little finger and laughed. "I've see yours, you tosser, and bet you wish you were an inch behind me" and he grabbed Jamie in a headlock. "Ok Egan you win". They both started laughing. "Good to have

you back mate, we've missed you".
"Thanks Buddy, same for me".

They grabbed some wine and headed for
Jamie's flat. "Hey Liam" Millie grabbed
him and flung her arms round his neck.
"Told you Jamie" "What did he tell you
Jamie?" they both laughed again and
Millie gave them that look that said 'I
guess I am not in the secret society'. "Sit
down boys, dinner is served". "Hey this
wine is really good Liam" "Thanks mate, I
read about in the Guardian last Sunday
while I was in Barbados" "Ok flash git!"
"Got yer again Jamie boy!" and they hi
fived one another. "You two are a bit
hyper active aren't you ok?" "Have you
told Liam our plans Jamie?" "What's this
intrigue then?" "We have decided to try
and start a family Liam and we wanted
you to be the first to know" "Hey that's
great news, pleased for you both" "Why
thank you Liam, we thought you would be
pleased".

"Now what about you, are you and Jayne
an item?" "Tell you what I love this meal
Millie" "Do I take that as a yes then?"

"No only joking Millie, we are just good mates and always will be. Poor Jayne got smashed on the last night. I did too but they took me to the room at eleven so I had more time to recover. I think it was something like 5.30am when Jayne got to bed so she was rough all the way home" "Oh poor Jayne she is such a lovely girl". "I did meet somebody though, near the end of the holiday and she gave me her phone number, so think I will meet her again". "What's her name Liam?" "Tracey Still, she has horse stables up in Derbyshire". "It sounds like a weekend break coming up in the Peak District, its beautiful Liam". "I had a great aunt who lived in Ackbourne which we used to visit every now and again when I was little".

"So how did you meet her?" "It was during a dancing competition that me and Jayne entered". "Still think Jayne has a secret crush on you Liam?" said Millie. "No, we are just good mates honestly".

"I know you are dying to ask me Millie?" said Liam, "Ask you what?" "About the dreams?" "I was hoping they had stopped for you" "No, quite the opposite, I know now that they are true, I have seen the places in the dreams" "You seem at peace with them now mate". "I am Jamie, I could tell you so much and to top it all Joan texted me today" "What? Liam showed Millie and Jamie the text from Joan. "She certainly is a girl of mystery Liam. You like all this intrigue don't you mate" "To be honest, I would like to be normal again but I have a feeling all this has an ending". "Well let's hope it's a happy one. Now who want some of my home made Bakewell Tart with clotted cream?" "Go on then honey" said Jamie. "What about you Liam?" "To be honest Millie, I think I will have an early night. I am knackered after the first day back at work" "Are you sure?" "Yes, but thank you and thank you so much for my favourite dinner" "Hey anytime you know that Liam". Liam gave Millie a kiss and shook hands with Jamie and left to get home for that early night.

Three months passed with no sign of another dream, it was the longest it had been. Liam had heard no more from Joan, but had contacted Tracey Still and she had invited him to stay at her house for a long weekend, Work was going really well and Liam was racking up some big bonuses. Even Jenny Fenney had been impressed. Liam had been out for a meal with Jayne, she had some pictures of the holiday that she had finally got round to getting printed for Liam to have copies. Jayne had without knowing taken quite a lot of pictures of Humphrey Slaley Morton's house and Jankay and Oday's bar.

Liam was home for 10.30pm that night, but was soon asleep, he had been working real hard and was thinking about the weekend coming up, when he would be in the Peak District in Derbyshire for the first time in his life.

That night the dreams started again. It had been two and half years since his brother in law Darrin Sumpt had died, leaving everything to his sister Kate.

Cabhan had saved a lot of money for his quest to be reunited with Jankay and Shona. What he didn't realise that night, was how sick his sister Kate really was. During the night of January 1635, Kate had been ill for almost four weeks with fever. One of the servants stayed with her every night but this night the wretched girl had fallen asleep. Kate had woken feeling thirsty, she really didn't know where she was and she fell down the great stairs breaking her neck. Cabhan was mortified, just when his life was turning for the better his sister died. Cabhan was now the sole heir to the fortune and knew that would mean another trip to London. What he didn't know, was the surprise awaiting him.

It was a bleak January day when he laid his beloved sister to rest in Claw Bay church. The Church had been built three hundred years earlier and its position on the cliff tops added to its mystery. It seemed to always be swirled in mist and on this day light flakes of snow had started to fall. There were only the servants and a handful of people from Claw Bay at the service. They sadly had their own problems and burials were common place due to starvation. With the estate in good order, Cabhan arranged his trip to London for the reading of his sisters will.

Cabhan arrived in London; it was no better a place than when he was last there. He decided to stay at the same boarding house, with its location being close to William Money's office. He didn't want the people who worked for Grapes seeing him in London. William Money had aged considerably since the last time Cabhan had seen him. He had an uncontrollable shake, which he tried to hide, but it was pretty bad. "Please take a seat Cabhan. Your sister didn't leave a will, so with you being the closest and sole relative, you will receive in full, your sister's estate". William Money then proceeded to give him maps of the land and the address of his bank where the money was held. "Good luck Cabhan and I am very sorry for your loss" he stretched out his weak thin arm and hand and with a lot of effort he shook Cabhan's hand. "Thank you Mr Money and good day to you Sir". Cabhan felt like a quick drink before he left for Ireland would be most appropriate. He avoided the Ale House he used last time, instead he chose the Blue Parrot in Crook Lane, just round the corner from Mr Money's office. The only thing he did right that day was to register the bank accounts and the land with the paperwork Money gave him. Once that was sorted it was time for the Ale House.

The whores were soon round Cabhan, he was a good looking man and money was no object at this time. One whore in particular, who was called Scarlett, made damned sure she got Cabhan drunk. When he woke up the next day, she had gone and his wallet too and there were three ugly looking men standing over him grinning. "Look what we have here lads, Mr Grapes will be pleased. You see Mr Cabhan, slaves don't run away from Mr Grapes, so you will be coming back with us and most possibly flogged to within an inch of your life before we string you up". Cabhan tried to reason with them saying it was mistaken identity. They were having none of it.

"Look, I have money; I can make you very rich men if you let me go" "Do you hear that lads, the Bog Arab here says he is rich? When have you ever seen a rich Bog Arab, hey boys?" They all laughed. Cabhan was a strong man, he had worked hard all his life and the only way out of this was to kill these mean, evil men stood in front of him. When the man released his last hand from the bed post, Cabhan took his chance. He grabbed a solid brass candle holder from the bedside table striking the first man across the throat. He went down immediately, the second man pulled a knife and Cabhan managed to spin him round killing the other man. That just left the one man who wasn't going to give up, so Cabhan launched at him sticking the knife right in his heart. Blood splattered everywhere. He stood for a few moments, which seemed like an age to Cabhan, and then he fell forward onto the other two. Now he had to get out of here. He quickly washed his hand, the blood swirling in the water carrier. He then headed straight for the bank and told them he had been robbed and any identification had gone. They didn't seem fazed, he was remembered by the bank manager and he didn't want to lose such an important customer. He gave Cabhan a thousand pounds from his account. Cabhan thanked them for their understanding and left for Ireland that night.

He was back in Claw Bay four days later; just as the sun was rising it was always a magical site, the sun rising over Claw Bay and the small shingle beach glistening in the impending sunrise.

Now he had a dilemma, if he tried to get back to Shona, Grapes will have heard about the men he had just killed or at least he thought that. Shona and Jankay were his only concern. He could not leave them rotting as slaves in the Caribbean now that he had all this wealth and position in society.

I woke again at 3.30am feeling frustrated. I wanted to know what would happen next but as was always the case, I fell back to sleep but no more dreaming!!

At work the following day, over lunch, Liam told Jamie what had happened on holiday and what his dream had told him. "Listen Liam, why don't we take a few days off and visit the West Coast of Ireland and let's see if the places you are dreaming about exist?" "I have looked on the internet Jamie and I can't find a Claw Bay" "Well maybe if we head out to County Mayo, we may find some history which will help you to figure all this out".

"Ok let's go this weekend" "That works great, Millie is away visiting her parents. Let me phone her up and she will book us a ferry crossing". Jamie called Millie. "Are you sure this is a good idea Jamie?" "Look, Liam seems a lot better since he came back from the cruise, so I think it helped him make sense of all this" "Ok I will call you back when I have something booked".

Friday morning the boys set off in Jamie's Range Rover Sport from Pembroke to Rosslare. They landed at 11.40am and they grabbed a map of County Mayo. They decided to drive across country to

LOOKING FOR SHONA

Galway, then take the coastal route North, hoping to come across Claw Bay at some point It was almost 4pm when they decide to get a bed for the night, at a small inn, in a town called McConlough Bay. They showered and changed meeting in the bar with the locals by 7.00pm.

It's very busy for a Friday night, the Guinness was flowing, and a man with a guitar and another man with a flute were playing all the Irish songs. Jamie being the most outward going person on planet earth got chatting to two old guys who were telling him stories about their days fishing. It was almost midnight when Ronnie, one of the guys, asked the boys how long they were staying, as he had enjoyed their company. "Well we are moving on in the morning, we are trying to find a small village on the coast called Claw Bay". The pub fell in silent. Ronnie got up touched his hat and left. The pub started emptying with the locals giving Jamie and Liam funny looks. "What did I say Jamie?" "Don't know mate, but it certainly freaked Ronnie and the rest of the pub". The landlord switched the light's off and said goodnight announcing at the same time that there was no breakfast served tomorrow, when only three hours earlier he had told the boys, that his pub did the best breakfast in County Mayo.

The only thing the boys could do now, was to go to bed, get up the next day and try and find Claw Bay if indeed it existed.

They left the pub at 9.30am the following morning. The landlord was nowhere to be seen so they left the monies for their rooms on the bar along with their room keys.

"Did you get the impression we upset somebody in there last night old lad?" "You bet we did Jamie". They travelled through quite a few villagers with strange names like, Groogy Hill and Down and Up Bay. The scenery was stunning. The coast road took them down a small track and just as they climbed up, Liam shouted "Stop!!" Jamie stopped the car, on the grass was a wooden sign, it just said 'Don't Enter' "It must be a private estate

Liam, come on lets crack on" "This is it Jamie, I know it this place, it's in my dreams" "Well we can't go any further in the Range Rover, we'd better walk".

Sure enough a house stood on the cliffs edge. "This is Tree Cliff Hall Jamie". Jamie looked bemused, it wasn't that he didn't believe his mate, just that he had only heard about these places when Liam would tell him about his dreams. The house was derelict. They tried to chop through the bramble and ivy to get to the door. Tree Cliff House had been a majestic piece of architecture Jamie thought, but now it was a shadow of what it must have been like. The roof was sagging inwards, the grounds were all overgrown. "Let's go inside Jamie". Liam pushed open the rotting oak door. Part of the grand staircase had fallen. "This is it Jamie, I could cry, I'm not going mental at all". They made their way to the outside garden. Liam ran to a tree in the grounds. "What is it Liam?" Suddenly Liam fell to the ground holding his chest, he was kind of frothing at the mouth. "Mate are you ok?" Liam was not coherent. Jamie pulled out his mobile phone but there was no signal. Jamie was panicking. There was only one thing for it, he had to try and get him to hospital. Jamie mustered up all the strength he had and carried his friend back up the hill to the car. He laid him on the backseat and put him on his side so he wouldn't choke. He suddenly remembered an App he had on his phone which found Emergency services. The App found Murray Hospital, which it said was eight miles away. He quickly pressed it into his Sat Nav. "Hang on mate, I will get you help". He drove like a mad man, eventually landing at the hospital two ambulance guys were stood outside smoking. Jamie shouted for their help, they came running over. Within five minutes Liam was in intensive care. Almost four hours passed before a nurse came and said that Liam was stable and he could go and sit with him. "What is the prognosis nurse?" "Doctor Mackay will talk to you in a short while" she said.

Jamie felt very upset, his best mate who had always been so healthy, looked dreadful he had pipes coming out of everywhere.

Almost an hour passed, when a thick set man in a white coat came in the room. Jamie stood up. "Are you the gentleman who brought Liam in?" "Yes, I am" he replied. "Son, your friend owes you his life, another ten minutes and there would have been nothing we could have done for him. He had a massive seizure and time really was important to him" "Will he be ok Sir?" "I am pretty confident he will be fine. Had he has had some kind of shock. What were the circumstances that led to his problem?" Jamie told Mackay about where they had been, he didn't say anything about the dreams that Liam had had.

"I have heard Claw Bay is not a place anybody goes too son. You are best not going there" "But why Mr Mackay?" "Sorry, I am a busy man" and he shook Jamie's hand and left.

What was it about Claw Bay that struck such fear into everyone? Jamie phoned

Millie and explained what had happened. "I told you not to go Jamie, there is something very odd and possibly evil happening in Liam's life" "This isn't connected Millie, he had a seizure" "I bet you it is Jamie, you just don't want to face it".

"Look never mind about that now, the main thing is to get Liam sorted. We could be here at least a week, depending on what they say. Maybe Liam should come to stay with us for a short while" "I agree Jamie, call me soon" "I will sweetheart, love you" "Love you too". The phone went dead and Jamie went back to the room. The nurse told Jamie he could have a bed in the hospital if he wished to be there for his friend. It was almost five days when eventually Liam's eye's opened. Liam speech was a little slurred but the nurse explained that he should be ok in a few days. "When can I take him home nurse?" "I would think the day after tomorrow, if the doctor is pleased with his progress" "Did you hear that Liam?" "What happened to me Jamie?" Jamie had to ask him to repeat what he had asked three times because of the slurred speech. Now do I tell him the truth or just say it happened somewhere else. He went for somewhere else he was frightened Liam would have another reaction.

It took Liam almost three months to recover from the seizure, in that time he never had a single dream. The doctor finally allowed him to return to work the following Monday and took him off the medication. Liam phoned Jamie to tell him the good news. "Hey mate that's great, so I am guessing you can have a beer tonight then with it being Friday?" "Yes mate where do you want to go?" "Well let's have a meal in Limey's then go onto Sticky Tina's, it's ages since I have had a dance Liam" "Ok mate anything for you, meet you outside Limey's at 5.30pm then".

Liam felt he should let Jayne know and he wasn't sure if he should let Tracey Still know too, but after some pondering he thought he would let them both know at the weekend.

Time seemed to be flying and Liam was just about to leave the flat when his phone rang. "Liam?" "Yes" "It's me, Joan" "Oh hello Joan, long time no speak" "I heard you had been poorly?" Liam brushed it off as if it were nothing, he didn't want Joan to be put off. "I think I owe you an explanation Liam. Can we meet?" "I am seeing Jamie tonight for a meal, then we are going to Sticky Tina's, you know where we met" "Can I meet you there please?" "Of course I will look forward to it Joan". The phone went dead so Liam left the flat and headed to Limey's. Jamie was stood outside waiting. "Where the hell have you been?" "Let's get inside and I will explain".

Syd, the waiter, took their coats. He knew Jamie quite well as he and Millie often ate at this restaurant.

"Right gent's, what can I get you to drink?" "Well I will have a French Martini" "And for you Sir?" Liam didn't look up; he seemed to be in a daze. "Liam you ok?" "Oh sorry I was miles away. I will have a Blue Moon with a slice of orange please". "Coming right up gents, take a look at the menus. On the special's tonight we have Welsh rarebit with red cabbage and a cream mustard sauce and we also have Salmon in a basil and Dill sauce with red wine cracked potatoes and a medley of garden vegetables. Right, I will be back in a minute".

"Are you ok Liam?" "Just got a lot on my mind Jamie, but I am fine" "What are you going to have and are we having a starter? I'm not bothered about a starter if I am going to be dancing later, what about you?" "No, thanks I'm fine". "There you go gentlemen, have you decided what you would like?" "Right, well I think I will have the Sliced Calves liver with Shallots in a pepper sauce with baby roast potatoes sprinkled with parsley and the vegetable medley please" said Jamie. "For you Sir?" Syd asked Liam. "Think I will have the Welsh rarebit from the specials menu please" "Ok thank you gentlemen" "Cheese on toast Liam?" "Ha, ha just because you are Mr Fancy Pants" "Say's Cruise boy!" and Jamie laughed.

"So come on then, what are you deep in thought about?" "Just as I was leaving the flat, I got a call from Joan" "What, *the* Joan?" "Oh yes" "Wow, what did she want?" "She wants to see me, she said she needs to explain" "When are you going to meet?" "Well hope you don't mind mate, but she is meeting me here at Sticky Tina's tonight. I know you like a dance so I hope you don't mind?" "Of course not mate, I would love it to work out for you. I will busy myself so won't be in the way". "Appreciate that mate. Thanks Jamie you are a good mate".

The meals came out. "To be honest mate, wish I'd have had the cheese on toast that looks lovely" "You will listen one day, Jamie boy".

It was 9.15pm when they entered the dark staircase leading into Sticky Tina's nightclub. There wasn't many in it was a bit too early. Within minutes of sitting down Joan came over to Liam's table and sat down. She looked stunning in a white dress with a thin leather belt round her waist and brown high heeled shoes. Joan was indeed a stunning black girl. Liam felt a bit nervous. "I feel like this is our first date Joan". Joan smiled her white smile lighting up every inch of her beauty.

They both tried to speak at once. "Sorry Liam, you go first". Liam cleared his throat, "After you didn't contact me, we, that's me and Jamie, saw you with that famous boxer going into a restaurant" Joan laughed, "So I am guessing you thought we were an item?" "Well it did look that way" "Well I can assure you we are not, I was doing some ambassador work and people like him give a lot of money to charity" "Ok so why did you contact me, then didn't see me and why would your friend say she didn't know you?" "Ok cards on the table time. I told my friend to say that if she ever saw you" "Why?" "Because what I am about to tell you may seem weird, but I believe it is true" "Go on then Joan, tell me".

"That night, in here, did you not think it odd that I came over to talk to you?" "Well I was flattered that you seemed to have chosen me" "Liam, please don't think I am crazy, but I was drawn to you and I am not sure why" "Well thanks". "No please, I'm not joking. Some months ago I returned from a visit to the Caribbean with work and from that day I have had dreams and the dreams are always the same, that I am a slave girl in Barbados". Liam was stunned, did he now tell her about him he thought. Liam tried to intervene. "Please Liam, hear me out. In the dreams I am a slave girl called Shona, which my real name of Joan is the equivalent name in English!!"

"The reason I am here today, is I saw you in a dream and I just know you have something in your past life that involves Shona..." "Why did you disappear Joan?" "Because I thought I was going crazy, but I now know you will understand" "I do very much understand. Can I ask you do you wake up from your dreams at a certain time?" "Yes, always at 7.10am. Why do you know the reason?" "No I don't, but I have the same dreams as you Joan and in my dreams I am in love with a black slave girl called Shona and when I wake up it's always 3.30pm".

"How much of this story do you know?" "I know I work in the laundry, in the big house and I know one of the Overseers was drunk and he and his boss, the big man Mister Grapes, raped me. Then they made me stand naked with my face against the wall and they fired shots at my head. They were so drunk they missed with each shot but Grapes got me in the shoulder. The scar Shona has, I have you have seen it on my shoulder". Joan showed Liam the mark on her shoulder again. "My granny used to tell me I had been marked to stay in this life".

"So where do we go from here Joan? Do you want to see me again or am I just a vehicle for your dreams?" "Please don't say that Liam, I feel a massive connection with you" "I'm sorry Joan, but I have been in a right mess, I will tell you in time but I was in Ireland recently, all because of these dreams and apparently I had a seizure so I have been ill for the last three months".

"Well Liam, I should be totally honest also, I have had the exact same thing. I decided to go Barbados on the pretence of a holiday and on the flight back I had a seizure". "Wow this is getting weirder by the minute. Do you think this is meant to be Joan? You see all my dreams are of Shona?" "Who are you in the dreams Liam?" "I am an Irish Slave called Cabhan". "You haven't figured in my dreams at all Liam, but I somehow keep getting this connection between us" "Have you tried any professional help?" "Yes it got so bad I had some regression sessions" "Did they work?" "Sort of, I also went on a cruise to the Caribbean and to Ireland, everything in the dreams I heard about or saw with my own eyes".

"I wonder why you are not figuring in my dreams Liam." "I honestly don't know Joan. Since my seizure I haven't had any dreams" "I haven't since mine either Liam".

"So where do we go now?" "Well now you know everything, I would like to carry on seeing you. Shall we start again Joan?" "I am so pleased you said that. Listen I can't be late tonight, I have a

conference call from America at home, so
need to be back at 10.00pm" "Ok Joan,
when are you free again?" "I will meet
you Saturday night at Lazlo's my treat".
"Don't be daft, I can't have a lady paying
for me" "Yes you can and you will" and
Joan laughed.

By the time Jamie came back, Joan had
left. "How did it go mate?" "Yeah we are
good, I'm seeing her Saturday night at
Lazlo's" "Great, shall me and Millie tag
along?" "If you don't mind mate, I'd
prefer it if you sat this one out, we have a
lot of catching up to do" "Ok, I know
when I'm not wanted Egan" "Thanks
mate, are you about ready?". The taxi
dropped Jamie off then Liam. Liam sat for
a minute by the river before going to his
flat. It was a crisp evening the nights were
starting to draw in. The full moon sat just
above the footbridge as if balanced on the
handrail majestically shining, it's light
across the river lighting up to make an
artificial walk across the river.

The beer was taking effect and Liam came
over tired, so he headed to the flat. He

poured himself a whisky and climbed in bed. Within minutes he was fast asleep and back in the world of Cabhan and Shona.

I was stood by the double doors that led onto the back garden, watching Mr Tibbles the gardener busying with his bee hives. It was then that I decided to grow a beard and my hair and dress like a Lord, that way Grapes would possibly not know me. It was a great risk, but one I had to take if I was ever to see my Shona and Jankay ever again.

I planned my trip for early November 1643, but in March 1642 the war in the North between the Protestants and the Catholics was gathering pace and land was burnt causing massive starvation. Many people fled to the West putting a strain on food resources in the villages. Cabhan had tried to help, if anyone knew about dire situations, it was Cabhan after what he had been through.

My estate manager Dermot Shingle knew of my dilemma but he also knew of my love for Shona. "Ye need to get away Sir and bring thy lady home to Ireland and settle down with some kids. That's just what that house needs" "I know I am just worried with all these troubles Dermot" "We will be fine Mr Cabhan" "If you are sure, then I must do this. I have decided to leave tonight for Barbados". The thought of seeing my lovely Shona again was filling me with apprehension and longing.

I took a boat to England then a ship from Liverpool to Barbados the arduous journey would take four months. I wrote in my diary every day. "We are six weeks into our journey and the weather is poor. We are being battered by high waves many people are sick, lucky for me I have a stomach that can stand most things".

"Day one hundred and nineteen. There was much excitement on board we could hear the sailors shouting land ahoy. Only that morning three dead bodies had been thrown overboard, I felt blessed yet again that I had made the journey".

LOOKING FOR SHONA

The ship docked and we disembarked. The Captain said he would sail for home in two weeks' time anyone not there would be left behind.

I purchased a buggy and headed for the Big House. The scene of some of my terrible memories but hopefully still the home of my beautiful Shona.

The long drive to the house brought back memories of my first day at the tender age of fourteen and the fear I felt. I had a plan that I would speak with Humphrey Slaley Morton on the pretence of looking to buy two girl slaves and see if he would sell them to me.

My buggy arrived in front of the white washed steps in front of the big house with its wrap round porch. A black slave dressed in a long blue velvet fishtail coat and beige jodhpurs with black buckled shoes. His hair was tied back with a yellow bow. "Can I help you Sir?" "I wish to speak to the owner of the house" "I am afraid Master Morton is too sick to talk to anyone". Suddenly a booming voice came from the side of the house, I knew that voice it was Grapes. "What can I do for you Irishman? Mr Grapes at your service" and he thrust his hand at me. Oh how I wanted to attack this man, I hated him so much, he was so cruel all the time.

Stay calm I thought. It was more important to get Shona out of there. My plan was to try and get Lomo's girlfriend out also. I owed Lomo that much. "I wondered Sir; do you have any slave girls to purchase? I will pay a good price for the right ones". I could see the greed in Grapes face. "Come into the house Sir, let us discuss over a taking of rum". This horrible man was running the house; the poor slaves were petrified of him. A boy, no older than twelve, spilt some rum he was shaking that much trying to serve us. Grapes jumped up and hit him with his cane across the head knocking the poor boy unconscious. "Get this heap of useless being out of my sight". The other four slaves stood at the door ran over and carried the poor boy out.

"Now then Mr?" "Oh sorry Sir, my name William Mires, I have bought a home in St Kitts and wish only the best servants. I really can't be bothered to go to auctions it is such a waste of my time". Grapes was studying me, I could feel his eyes burning into my face. "So Mr Grapes, I need two girls for my laundry and I want experience". "Just sold one two months ago, she was a trouble maker, so had to go but I have five I can show you, but could only sell you one Sir, if the money was right of course". "For sure Mr Grapes, I understand". Damn I thought, that would mean leaving Lomo's girl behind unless I could offer him something ridiculous.

Grapes barked out some orders and the five girls were brought up from the laundry. Grapes had them stood in a line; they bowed their heads clearly petrified of this man. He pulled the first one from the line. "This is Missy Alvita, show Mr Mires your teeth". The poor girl obeyed Grapes, he then made her strip off her top. "See Mr Mires she is good stock, aren't you Alvita?" The poor girl just nodded. Grapes then grabbed the next one it was

Lomo's girl Aoi. "This is Missy Aoi, she can be feisty but a little whipping sorts that out doesn't it?" Aoi nodded. "Show the good man your teeth". "Mr Grapes, just the teeth will be fine they don't need to strip". "Whatever you want Mr Mires, but I always like to look at my enjoyment before I buy". I could feel the anger inside me. He carried on down the line. "Is that it?" "Yes, like I said I sold one not long ago. You would not want her she was trouble Mr Mires; we are well shut off her".

The other three girls were not Shona, so I could only assume Shona was the one sold. "How much for Missy Aoi?" "I thought you would like that one, ten Kings Shillings". I didn't want to sound too keen so I haggled and we eventually decided on eight shillings. Grapes though he had done well. They put Aoi in the buggy, just as I was about to leave Grapes looked at me. "Sure I don't know you Sir? I never forget a face" he then turned and went back to the porch. My heart was racing, but at least I had Aoi and she could help me find Shona.

LOOKING FOR SHONA

Once we were out of sight, I stopped the buggy. Aoi looked terrified. "Aoi it's me Cabhan" "Cabhan?" and she flung her arms round me. "Where is Shona, Aoi?" "Sorry to tell you this, Grapes raped her and made me watch, she fought back and tried to get away but he shot her. It lodged in her shoulder. But Grapes was satisfied, so he was just laughing. She was writhing in pain but he carried on and finished raping her then he laughed and walked away. We managed to get the lead ball out of her shoulder and dress her but she had lost a lot of blood. We covered for her the best we could but after a month Grapes men came and took her to be sold at market" "Which market?" "The one in Bridgetown where me and Lomo used to go with Grapes?" "Yes I think so" "Let's get down there" "What are you going to do with me?" "I intend to find Shona and my friend Jankay and take them back to live in Ireland with me. I have wealth and I would like you to come also" "Can we find Lomo?" This was going to be the hardest thing I had ever done. "Lomo died Aoi, he was very brave". Aoi started crying uncontrollably. I put my arm round her and comforted her. I hope one day these people understand what their actions did to people's lives. One day history will know I thought.

We arrived in Bridgetown and I spotted the guy who did the sales when I was forced to go with Lomo and Grapes. "Stay here Aoi". "Good afternoon, good fellow". The tall slightly tanned Auction master was taken back by my approach. "What do you want?" "I am wishing to buy another slave girl for my laundry on St Kitts. I have one girl I have just bought and she said her friend, who goes by the name Shona, would be ideal, but I do believe she was sold not long ago" "I know her, very pretty but very feisty she had a wound on her shoulder so the price was lower than she would have normally been sold for".

"I wondered kind Sir; could you tell me who bought her?" I pressed two shillings into his grubby hands. "She is on St Kitts; well at least that's where she was sold too. A Plantation called Latte on the north of the island". "Well thank you, kind Sir. Oh before I go, Mr Grapes at the Morton House, told me he sold a slave called Jankay, some years back and he said he would make a good fighter for me".

"Can't remember him". I again pressed two shillings in his hand. "It's coming back to me; he was a Mountain of a man. Let me think" I pressed another two shillings in his hands I wanted off the island in case Grapes had worked out who I was. "He was sold to the Brownlow plantation, but that's a good few years ago". "Well thank you for your information Sir" and I touched the brim of my hat. I could sense he also knew who I was but could not quite work it out.

I hired a boat and we got across to St Kitts. It was nightfall, so I stopped at a ramshackle bar and asked for a couple of rooms. The man in his early seventies said my room was one shilling, but the nigger girl would have to sleep with the horses. I had no choice but to go along with it.

I made sure Aoi was ok, I bought her some food, some clothes and shoes for her feet. The next day was going to be challenging I thought.

I woke at 7.00am and fetched Aoi from the stables. The inn keeper was pottering about. "Do you have a buggy I can have on loan from you for a few days Sir?" "It will be two shillings a day I might add" "That's fine, I will take five days.

I was all set now to find my beautiful Shona. We eventually found the Latte Plantation. Pulling up outside the Grand House I was met by a man in his finery. "Can I help you good Sir? Alexander Pilkington, at your service". "William Mires Sir, and my slave girl, Missy Aoi". "Take the girl with the horse; come into my parlour Mr Mires". "Would you mind feeding my slave girl?" "Of course not" Pilkington told one of the slaves to feed Aoi.

"Whisky or Rum Sir?" A small rum please, Mr Pilkington". Pilkington handed me a tumbler full of rum. "How can I help you Sir?" "Well it's like this, I need two good girls for my laundry, I have one and she said the best girl she worked with was a girl called Shona, who I believe you may have purchased from Barbados Sir" "Possibly, but I leave the staffing to my wife Elisabeth Pilkington" "Darling do you have a minute to meet my guest?". A stunning lady dressed in a flowing yellow dress came in and shook my hand. Pilkington explained about Shona. "I don't give them names, I number them, and so I would have to introduce them all to you". Quickly thinking I asked them to bring Aoi. I didn't want them knowing I knew Shona. Twelve girls in total came up, most looked like they were well treated, the last one up didn't, and it was my Shona. She didn't look up, but Aoi in her excitement ran to her. "Get back" Pilkington barked. Aoi retreated back, bowing and scraping as she did. I just managed to put my finger to my mouth to tell Shona not to say anything. Pilkington spotted this. I then made out I was pondering. "Is this the girl Missy Aoi?" "Yes Master, that is Shona the best laundry girl" "Ok, how much would you take for her?" "She isn't for sale Mr Mires" "Everybody has a price and to be honest the others look a lot better". Sensing my need Pilkington's wife said fifteen shilling.

I didn't want to look too keen and we settled on twelve shillings. We drove away in the buggy with the two girls in the back my heart was pounding; poor Shona looked malnourished so my next stop was an inn.

"You can't bring those in here" the inn keeper said, looking at the two girls so we had to sit outside. The meal came and the inn keeper looked at me strangely having never seen this before.

I cuddled Shona, it was the best feeling I had ever had, and I just needed to get Jankay now. "Do either of you know where Jankay is?" The inn keeper overheard the name. "The big nigger you looking for? I believe his old Master bought him back, he had won every fight on St Kitts and because of that the rich people were worried he would become a leader for the slaves, so it was decided he was to be sold and a Mr Grapes bought him from Barbados. Why do you ask about him?" "I want the best fighter for myself" "Well he is certainly that Sir". "Thank you good fellow, can we have two rooms?" "I can't let the niggers have their own rooms they, can go with the horses. If, of course, you want to be entertained by them, they can come to your room Sir". "Ok I will take one room, but I want good bedding for my girls". "Consider it done Sir" said the inn keeper. Cabhan showed the girls to the stables, "Will you be ok Aoi?" "Yes thank you Cabhan" "I am pleased you and Shona have found each other". Shona had been quiet and when they got to the room she broke down crying.

I hugged her like I was never going to let her out of my sight ever again. She finally stopped crying. "I thought I would never see you again Cabhan" she sobbed. "I promised I would return for you". "But before I can fully be with you, I need to tell you I was raped by Mr Grapes, he did this in front of Aoi" "I will kill him Shona" "No we must not go back there. Aoi said you are taking us to Ireland". "I am a very rich man now Shona, we can go back to my birthplace and have a family you will never be cold and hungry again my love". She squeezed me. "Do you still want me after Grapes has done this to me". "My darling, I have come many miles to get you back, we will always be together, until the end of time we will never be parted again I promise you".

That night they passionately embraced each other, exploring every part of each other. This was so different than when they were forced together to try and make a child, this was pure love, two people becoming one.

"I love you so much Cabhan, when will we go to Ireland?" "I am going to leave you here and go back to Barbados to get Jankay. I can't leave him in that hell hole Shona" he replied. "Please be careful my love, my heart is with you".

That morning I sailed back to Barbados, I met with the ship due to return to Liverpool the captain agreed to stop off at St Kitts, so I could pick up Shona and

Aoi. I told the Captain I would be back in twenty four hours and then we could sail.

I drove back to the Morton house in the little black buggy. Grapes greeted me. "What they done, run away? Well you ain't having no money back Mr Mires" and he laughed. I hate this man more than anything I have ever known. I want to send him to hell but first I have to find Jankay.

"Mr Grapes, how wonderful to see you again, the girls are fine my man servant is looking after them". "Then why do we have your pleasure again?" "To be honest I was at an inn on St Kitts and the inn keeper was telling me all about the famous black fighter, Jankay. Well I wondered if you would be willing to sell him to me. I want to take him round the islands to fight it's a great sport" "Not sure you could afford Jankay, Mr Mires" replied Grapes. "Let me see the specimen and let's see if I can be persuaded". Grapes clapped his hands, "Get Jankay and Labron up here now". The servant ran away and returned a few minutes later

luckily Jankay didn't recognise me he had
aged and his hair had started turning grey.

"What say we have a little wager? One
hundred shillings says Labron will kill
Jankay. If Labron wins then you have no
Jankay and I get the wager if Jankay wins.
I get one hundred shillings and you get
Jankay. But before you agree, I want
Jankay's left arm strapped to his body to
make the fight fair". "Hardly seems fair
Mr Grapes" I said. "Jankay is feared
throughout the islands, but not feared as
much as me hey Jankay? Show Mr Mires
how I keep you in check". Jankay turned
round his body was lacerated with deep
cuts on his back that had healed and had
been opened again.

I had to agree to Grapes' terms and I
hoped my friend was still capable of the
task ahead. The money was put down on
the table and Grapes looked like he was a
man obsessed with the infliction of pain as
they strapped Jankay's arm to his body.
Let them fight to the death. Before
Jankay could get off his chair, Labron
launched at him kicking him in his private

parts. Labron was kicking and screaming, he bit Jankay like a crocodile then he tried to gouge his eyes.

They rolled about a lot, Jankay seemed to have given in, all the beatings from the past appeared to have taken their toll on his body, although his body was magnificent, his will had gone. Labron bit a piece of Jankay's ear and spit it out this man was vicious. A bell sounded and they stopped. "Still want to carry on Mr Mires?" Grapes laughed. Did he know who I was I wondered? What choice do I have, poor Jankay's life was miserable anyway, if he could just muster enough strength I could get him out of this hell hole? I had no choice I leant over him and whispered in his ear, "It's me, Cabhan; I have come to take you away". Jankay suddenly realised who I was and ran at Labron with one almighty blow he knocked Labron off his feet and stood over him. "He has to kill him to win Mr Mires", sneered Grapes. I could see in Jankay's eyes that he didn't want to do that. "What if I buy the pair Mr Grapes?" I offered. "I would take 240 shillings and not a penny less". I agreed to save my friend.

"Ok release the pair of them, put them in Mr Mire's buggy". The room emptied and Grapes looked at Cabhan, coming very close, so close that Cabhan could smell the rancid smell of sweat on his body. "Thank you for the money Sir. Oh and thank you for the laundry maid that you came looking for" "I'm sorry?" I said, "I know who you are Mires". I knew in that instance I had to react, I grabbed Grapes round the throat we tussled on to the floor knocking over a lamp and I slowly choked him to death. His eyes rolled into the back of his head as he took his last breath on this earth. I felt only elation at killing this man who had made all our lives pure hell on earth.

I bundled Grapes into a cupboard and picked up the two hundred and forty shillings and left. I knew we probably only had one hour before he was found, so with great haste we headed for the port. Jankay and Labron, who by now had come round, were asking me questions.

"Let me get us on the ship bound for Ireland and your freedom, before they come after us". "Why will they come after us, you paid for us?" "I did but then I murdered Grapes and picked up the money". For the first time Jankay laughed I had never seen him so happy.

We made it to the ship in good time, I told the captain I would pay him an extra two hundred shillings to leave now which he agreed. We landed in St Kitts and picked Aoi and Shona up. On the boat we didn't speak much, for fear the Captain would turn us in. It was a long four months, but we final landed in Liverpool. The joy on Shona's face was magical, she was my dark princess her beauty glowed and shone at everyone she met.

I was feeling a little more comfortable now as we left Liverpool for Ireland and eventually Claw Bay. A few days later we arrived at Tree Cliff house, I introduced my friends, although some of the staff seemed somewhat amused by the colour of my friend's skin.

LOOKING FOR SHONA

I awoke at 3.30am yet again. I could remember everything and could not wait to see Joan to tell her that Cabhan and Shona were safe and maybe now our lives would be complete.

I had no more dreams, but Saturday could not come quick enough. I arrived at Lazlo's, Joan was sat at the bar, her long legs dangling from the stool her perfect formed body sitting snugly in the bar chair. How lucky am I. Joan turned and stood up planting a long lasting kiss on my lips.

"If you would like me to show you to your table, Sir, Madam. Can I ask is this a special occasion?" I quickly turned to the waiter and said "Yes I have found my Shona" Joan giggled and the waiter smiled, thinking I am some kind of nut case. The beautiful food was secondary to our conversation as we held each other's hands and I told the whole story to Joan. It would have sounded far-fetched if she had not also have had some of the same dreams.

We finished the meal, I paid the bill and we headed out into the night. "Do you want to walk back Joan? And will you be staying at mine? Sorry, I hope I am not being presumptuous" "Of course I am staying the night. I don't want to leave you ever. Listen one of the reason I didn't want you knowing where I live was because then you may have wanted to stay and these dreams were frightening me" she said shyly.

"You just seemed like a mystery girl" and Liam laughed. "Sorry I didn't mean to be" replied Joan. That night they made passionate love. Their passion and lust for each other, creating the feeling equal to that of an erupting volcano, inside both of them. They finished exhausted and lay holding each other tightly, as if to carry on the feeling of fullness forever. "I am in love with you Liam" whispered Joan, "Well that's a good job, I am in love with you Joan" "Is it just me or do you feel this warmth between us, as if we have been together forever?" "Yes I do Joan, I used to curse the dreams in the beginning, now I believe they have pulled us together and

I could not be happier. I hope Cabhan and Shona feel the happiness I feel right now Joan".

Time moved on, both Joan and Liam were no longer having dreams they had been engaged for almost four months. Joan had moved in with Liam, the only minus point was that Joan still did a lot of travelling in her job, which meant Jamie dragging Liam round the bars quite often after work.

It was one of these nights that Jamie surprised Liam, while they were dining at Jamie's favourite restaurant Sapori D' Italia. "These meatballs are the best Liam" "Don't let Millie hear you say that" "How are you two? Sorry I have not been round but every spare minute I have, I try and spend with Joan?" "I've noticed, it must be love mate" "I think I am going to ask her to marry me Jamie" "Oh that's great news mate" "Will you be my best man?" "You try stopping me Egan. Where will you propose to her?" "I wondered about taking her to Ireland, to see if we can find Cabhan and Shona's house". Jamie felt very concerned, how he could tell his mate that the seizure took place there, after he had told him a completely different story.

"Do you not think you are best letting the past, stay in the past mate? This is a new life for you both". "I hear what you are saying, but my dreams were so much more intense than Joan's. I have shared mine with her and the connection with Tree Cliff House is strong Jamie. I could probably get a license to marry my Joan there". "I'm sure she would much prefer to be married on a beach in Sri Lanka more though mate, or what about Vegas? The girls could go to Los Angeles for a few days, we could have the stag party in Vegas, then Joan and the rest of the girls could come down for the wedding at the little White Chapel that Elvis married at? Go on mate, I am excited at that thought and remember it will be your last taste of freedom and what happens in Vegas stay's in Vegas" and Jamie laughed.

"I need to propose to her first Jamie, she might say no" "Don't be daft, she is nuts

about you, even Millie said that" "I think
we might go to York for a long weekend
and I might ask her in the Cathedral"
"Wow, I like that idea buddy". "Ok, well I
will let you know where we are going to
get married, if she accepts my proposal".
They left the restaurant and as usual Jamie
was on top form "Oh Las Vegas the devil"
he was singing all the way to the taxi rank.
The little cockney cabbie looked at Liam.
"Is your bladdy mate on something
governor?" "Only Italian meatballs mate,
he thinks we are going to Vegas and he
loves to party" "You need to watch him,
he will get you locked up my son" "Hey
don't you be sick in my Cab matey",
driver said to Jamie. "I'm fine, just happy
for my mate". The cabbie turned round
and never spoke again until finally
dropping Jamie first at his apartment, then
Liam at his. "Good luck with your Fruit
Loop mate old son". The cabbie
disappeared down the road and Liam
made his way upstairs to the apartment.
He checked his phone for messages. There
were fifteen in all, all from Joan.
Apparently she had been trying to ring
me, he looked at his mobile but the battery

was flat. It was too late to phone Joan now.

'I do love that girl' he thought to himself. Liam decided to look at weekend breaks in York, he found one staying in the Shambles at the hotel Turpin, it said it was near the centre of York with parking and en-suite rooms with a Jacuzzi. 'First thing tomorrow I am going to book that' he thought. He cleaned his teeth and feeling happy with his life he fell asleep.

The dream started again. "Cabhan what do you want us to do my friend?" "Do what you want, I am a very rich man you Aoi and Labron can just enjoy your lives, I have boats you can go fishing. If you want to work in the garden, it is huge and there is everything here for you to enjoy your life. Grapes, or any of those other bastards, will never be in our lives again my friend. Tomorrow I will take you all to town for new clothes and shoes".

"Thank you Cabhan, how will I ever repay you?" "It is me that owes you a debt my friend, I will never let you down" and

LOOKING FOR SHONA

Jankay and Cabhan hugged. "I am jealous" said Jankay, "Miss Shona, your beauty is beyond compare and I am just an ugly man" and he laughed. Aoi looked at Jankay. Jankay felt her eyes on him and he smiled at her.

The following morning Cabhan hitched up the buggy for the fourteen mile drive into Timmid, the nearest town to Claw Bay. When they arrived outside the tailors there were gasps of amazement from some of the local town folk. One little boy shouted to his friend "Look that big man needs a wash, he is blacker than you Rory" The boy's mother slapped him across the head and apologised to Cabhan's party. "I am sorry for my sons ignorance he ain't ever seen a black face be for Sir!!!"

"Apology accepted dear lady" said Cabhan. Jankay just looked at the boy with his big eyes which made the little boy run to get under his mum's petticoat. "Think you did a good job there Jankay" said Labron. "Only having some fun with him" replied the big man. They entered the shop and the Tailor and his assistant were also taken back by the four black people with Cabhan.

"I wish you to serve my friends with four suits for the men with four shirts, socks and four pairs of shoes each, my good man. And for the ladies Sir, a dozen of your finest dresses, show them what you have Sir"

The tailor started bringing out all these dresses, but Cabhan could see he was alarmed by the whip marks on all of them. "Were you in an accident?" he naively asked. "Something like that" they told him. Shona came out in a blue dress and bonnet she looked magnificent, Cabhan was holding back tears of joy.

"Sir. Who is the priest here, in Timmid?" Cabhan asked the tailor, "That will be Mr Ross Sir" "Where might I find Mr Ross?" "He is just across the street Sir". "You carry on sorting my friends, and I will be back soon". Cabhan walked across the muddy road and knocked on the black door. "Enter and tell me your business", came the reply. "My name is Cabhan and

I wish to speak to you priest". "Enter my son". Mr Ross was a lanky man, about six foot three, with straggly blonde hair thinning on top. "Now what's your business Mr Cabhan?" "I wish to be married?" "Do you now and who to may I ask?" "The lady in question is Shona" "What a beautiful name where in Ireland is she from Sir?" "County Mayo, same as us" was the reply. "Whereabouts Mr Cabhan" "We live at Tree Cliff house Mr Ross" "I hope you are not suggesting you live over the brush Mr Cabhan?" "No Sir most definitely not, she lives in one part of the house and I live in the other" "I know where you live now, I married Miss Kate and Mr Darrin Sumpt in the little chapel overlooking Claw Bay in the grounds of Tree Cliff House. They were a lovely couple, it was so sad for Kate when Mr Sumpt died. Did you acquire the property from Kate Sumpt then Mr Cabhan?" "No I am afraid my sister passed away and she left the house to me" "Oh Kate was your sister, I am sorry I didn't know she had left this life", and he bowed his head with respect making the cross sign across his chest.

"If you and your bride to be would like to come to see me on Wednesday of next week, we can make arrangements Mr Cabhan" "Mr Ross, just call me Cabhan". "Ok, as you wish, Cabhan".

I was feeling quite pleased with myself, life was at last, sweet. My sister had left me well provided for, I had helped my friends escape the hell that is slavery and I was going to marry the women I love. I felt blessed.

Once back at the tailors shop, everyone looked well in their respective finery, but my Shona looked like a princess, she could have graced and Royal family. I settled the bill with the tailor and we loaded the buggy with our purchases for the drive back to Claw Bay.

Just listening to everyone laughing and being happy, was more than enough of a payment for me, after the dreadful life they had led. Jankay and Labron had decided they would like to work in the gardens, they didn't have to, but they said they would feel better if they paid for their keep. Aoi asked if she could help in the laundry and even my Shona wanted to work, but I explained the lady of the house didn't work. I'm not sure she understood fully my sentiments but I would not let her work.

I tossed and turned and woke at bloody 3.30 am again. It was a bit of a shock to find Joan fast asleep beside me. I had remembered leaving Jamie and the cabbie kicking off about him being so loud. I can't remember anything else. I went to the bathroom there was ice on the windows, it felt cold. From the beam of the street light, I could see small white flakes falling. I made my way through the living room and opened the sliding doors leading on to the balcony. It had snowed heavy in the night. I felt like I had lost time.

Suddenly I felt a hand on my shoulder. "Good morning my darling, how are you?" "I'm good Joan, what day and date is it?" "It's Boxing Day. We are going to the Christmas celebrations at Somerset House, do you not remember?" "Joan this is really weird, all I can remember is leaving Jamie in a taxi and the cabbie banging on about Jamie being so loud. When I got to the flat I had a dream again and I can remember all that for my diary!!" "That was almost five months ago, can you not remember anything since then at all?" "No Joan I can't" "Sit down let me makes us a coffee".

Liam sat down on the cream leather suite trying to piece together the events of the last five months. Joan came back and started to piece together the missing time for Liam. "Well first things first, you had promotion at work." "Really? above Jamie?" "No, you both got promoted. Jenny Fenney got promoted to the board, so they felt it was too much work for one person and so they split the job and you were both promoted. That same day you phoned me and asked me to move in with you, so here I am that was about three months ago. Since then I have changed my job and I work for UNICEF, but I am based in London with only the very odd trip abroad. Your friend Glofachs had his life support machine switched off two months ago. You went to the funeral and Jamie did a speech". "Oh Joan how dreadful, I can't remember any of this". "Lots happened but mostly irrelevant". "Have you had anymore dreams Joan?" "No funnily enough, but every morning I wake at exactly 7.10 am for some reason". "Have I seemed odd at all?" "No Liam, you have been very happy, you have booked for us to go to York on the 29th December for four days". "I remember something about that I wonder why? Let me tell you what happened in my dream". It took almost two hours for Liam to relive his dream. It was now 9.15am. "Come on Liam we said we would meet Jamie and Millie at Future Coffee in Covent Garden at 10.30 am".

Liam showered and shaved, looking in the shaving mirror he thought to himself that his dream life was the life he craved and he was convinced that Joan was Shona and of that he had no doubt.

It took Liam and Joan thirty five minutes to walk to Covent Garden. With the snow on the ground it made hard going. The trees lay heavy with their quilts of white snow hanging precariously to the branches. Jamie and Millie were sat in the window seat, looking out at the children throwing snowballs at each other and any unsuspecting tourists who passed by.

"Morning you two, sit down I will get you a coffee. What would you like Joan?" "Can I have a Gingerbread Latte, please Jamie?" "Just an Americano for me please mate". The girls were soon in conversation. Jamie returned armed with the coffee order. "So what time are you two heading up to York?" and he winked at Liam. Liam clearly didn't know why he winked at him. "We will set off at lunchtime on Wednesday and we are staying for four nights". So, you'll not be seeing in the New Year with your mate then". "Give over Jamie, they are in love, like we were once!" and Millie laughed. "Right now the coffees are drunk, are we going round the Christmas fayre? I want to have a go at ice skating, Millie will you do it with me?" "Love to Joan, what about you boys?" "No ta, we will be in the Bull and Badger, we can watch from there,

Directors bitter in hand" "Waste of space you two" "What Millie isn't telling you Joan, is that she was Home Counties Ice Skating Runner Up two year's running when she was fifteen" "Really Millie?" "Yes, I've done quite a bit of ice skating". "You can teach me then mate, I am like Bambi, but I enjoy it and that's all that matters".

The boys found The Bull and Badger and a seat near the window, while the girls enjoyed ice skating. "Joan wasn't joking about being Bambi was she? Whoops down she goes again" "At least she's had a go mate" "Oh I know, only pulling your leg Liam. So have you decided on a date for the wedding and more importantly are we going to Vegas for the wedding and stag do?" "Who's wedding?" questioned Liam. "Yours, of course. Knob head!" "Am I getting married?" "What do you mean?" "That was the idea of going to York; you said you were going to propose to her in York Cathedral!!"

Liam came clean about the last few months. Jamie was shocked. "You have been so happy mate, in fact the best I have ever seen you" "Do you know something Jamie; I love my dreams, if that's what they are. But I am worried that I look to be functioning normally to you and everyone else, but I have no recollection of the last few months". "Well trust me mate, you have been outstanding at work and you are clearly keeping Joan happy so things are not that bad".

"Jamie, I have a diary. I keep it in my backpack in my wardrobe, should anything ever happen to me I would like you to have it". "Stop being so miserable you are younger than me. I know you don't look it though" and Jamie laughed. "Seriously Jamie too many funny things have happened since the night with the Ouija Board, that I am not sure what to expect next". "Mate, don't go down that route" "Ok explain it to me? We go to Ireland and I have a seizure. My dreams take me to the Caribbean. I go with Jayne and I am physical sick at one historic stop. My dreams relate to all these places. In fact you never did tell me where I had my seizure?". Jamie still felt he could not tell

Liam where, so his reply was not the truth. "We were on our way back to the ferry mate".

"Joan is the double of Shona in my dreams. I have never told you this, but Joan had dreams as well, not as many as me and not as vivid, plus she feels a connection with me" "I wondered why she fancied an ugly buggar like you" and he laughed. "Bollocks Trench!!" "Only joking Bud, am I still your best man?" "Of course, now that I know I am going to ask her".

"Shut up, they are here". The girls came in giggling and laughing. "That was great fun Liam, you should have come, Millie is so good aren't you Millie?" "Well I practised a lot as a kid Joan" "Right are you two ready? We want to see the Christmas Fayre and market. These two will sit in here all day won't you boys?" "As if Millie?" and they laughed as they put their coats on ready to go out into the crisp winter's afternoon.

"Hey Liam come and look at this" Joan had found a big Coney fur hat "Get it if you want it. It could be cold in York, tha' knows it gets bitter up North" "Was that supposed to be a Yorkie accent Liam?" "Why? Can you do one better Trench?" Jamie started his Yorkshire accent. "You sound more like bloody Adam Faith instead of Geoff Boycott" "Come on you two let's have a go at the darts" "What do we have to do?" "You have to throw two darts out of three through Santa's mouth and whatever the dart hits on the way down you win" "What can you win?".

The guy on the stall had on a woolly jumper that had seen better days and a bobble hat with no bobble, he said "You can win things like watches, rings, bracelets, a tenner and selection boxes" "How much do you want mate?" "It's five pounds for three darts" "We'd better have four lots of three darts then". First up was Liam. One dart went in Santa's mouth and two landed in his cheek. Next up was Millie; she got all three darts in Santa's mouth and won a Mars selection box. "Yummy" said Jamie, "Keep your eyes off Jamie, I will be consuming these whilst I am watching the Only Fools and Horses Christmas Special in my Jim Jams" "What are Jim Jams Millie?" "Sorry Joan, my PJ's" she corrected herself. Joan still looked confused. Liam shouted "Pyjamas" "Whoops silly me, sorry" they all fell about laughing. Jamie had no joy with the darts and now it was Joan's turn. Joan scored two through the Jolly Santa's mouth and won a watch. "I will treasure this Liam" and she laughed. They left the Fayre, the girls with their prizes and the lads with their tails between their legs.

"Well that was a really enjoyable afternoon, why don't you two come to us for dinner Millie". "Sorry Joan, Boxing day is a ritual in our house. I sit on the sofa watching Only Fools and Horses, Coronation Street and the Eastenders Christmas Specials, with my feet draped over poor Jamie, while he feeds me chocolate until I want to burst" "You will have the same little ritual's once he makes an honest woman of you Joan". Jamie looked at Liam and they both smiled.

"Right me and Millie are having a taxi back, are you sharing?" "No mate we are going to have a steady walk back along the river" "Ok will see you both in the New Year, thanks for a great afternoon" "You too, we've both had a lovely time and Joan now has an expensive watch that can colour your wrist when you wear it, so it's a magic watch as well" Joan clipped Liam round the head. "You boys are only jealous because we girls whipped your asses".

Millie and Jamie waved as they drew away in the taxi. "What a lovely couple Liam, you have such nice friends" "They are your friends now Joan" he said. Joan snuggled into Liam as they strolled along the riverbank back to the flat.

Once back at home and in the warmth, they settled in to tee shirts and track suit bottoms. Joan made roast potatoes, onion rings, celery and cream cheese sticks. There was some pork pie and some small beef wellington's she had bought from Harrods. "What do you fancy watching?"

"You decide Liam" "What about something on Netflix's?" "Fine by me".

This looks good, he said "Ten Years a Slave". "Are you sure Liam?". "Look we both have to face this or it will never end" "Ok if you are sure". Liam hardly spoke for the two and three quarter hours that the film was on.

"What did you think Joan?" He hadn't noticed but Joan had been crying. "Hey, come here, what is it?" "Oh nothing, it's just me being silly Liam" "Come on you can tell me" "I just don't want to ever lose you Liam, and watching that, I got a couple of flash backs to my dreams" "What did you see?" "I saw you manacled" "Does Cabhan look like me Joan?" "I have never been able to remember until now. Yes he is your double from what I see" "Does Shona look like me Liam?" "Yes she is almost identical; you are maybe a bit taller".

"Why do you think you will lose me?" "I don't know I just feel it", said Joan sadly. "You won't ever cheat on me Liam, will you?" "No of course not" "I have to ask you this, but the other week when you were out with Jamie, I took a call from somebody called Tracey Still. She left her number, when I asked you about it, you said it was nothing and brushed it off can you remember?" "Sorry, no I can't. I met Tracey on the cruise with Jayne and she said she would call me so I could go riding at her stables in Derbyshire, but then you came back into my life, so I never contacted her and that is all Joan. We had never even been out together". "Sorry Liam, it's just sometimes everything seems so complicated".

"Come here silly, I love you, don't you ever forget it?" "I know, I love you too" "Right, let's watch Emmerdale, seeing as how we are going to York" "Oh I have never watched it, but the girls drool over Cain Dingle" "Jamie thinks he looks like Cain Dingle, Joan" "Well Jamie is a good looking man". "Steady on there girl, no exaggerating in my house" and Liam laughed.

"Hey, is that him?" said Liam pointing to the TV. "Yes that's Cain, Jamie does look a bit like him round the eyes Liam" "Don't bloody tell him that! He always wants to morph into whatever setting he is in. When we go to the Italian, he thinks he looks like a young Al Pacino!!" "Really? He doesn't look anything like him, Mel Gibson perhaps" and she laughed and Liam hit her with a cushion.

A couple of days later they were off to York. "I have never been to York Liam. New Year's Eve I want to go into York Minster. They have a Ferris wheel too, shall we do that also?" "Why not, it's a take on the London Eye I believe". "I checked the hotel on Trip Advisor and it's got excellent reviews". The Turpin, named after the famous Highway Man arrested in York, was a five star hotel, just off the cobbled streets of the Shambles. "This is beautiful Liam, thank you" "It's only beautiful because I have the most beautiful girl in the whole world on my arm" "Ahhhh you are so sweet Mr Egan". They booked into the hotel. For such and old hotel it was in excellent condition with very helpful staff. "You can see how they get such great reviews on Trip Advisor Liam" "I have booked us into a restaurant in the Shambles for 8.00pm so we should make a move".

The Lamplight Library was a small intimate restaurant. From the outside there hung a traditional pub sign, in cream. The writing simply said "The Lamplight Library Restaurant". The two bowed windows at the front, had net curtains, which were draped and tied back, candles flickered in the window casting small shadows on the sprinkle of snow on the ground. There were six curved steps leading up to the door which was also painted cream to match the sign. They were met by the front of house lady. She was in her mid-forties with her hair in a ponytail, dressed in all black with a white blouse. "Good evening, welcome to the Library. May I take your coats?". We removed our coats and were shown into a room with oak bookshelves all around the perimeter of the room. The book shelves heaved with the amount of books on display.

"May I take your drink order please?" she asked Liam. "Could we have a bottle of Hugel ET Fils 1977 vintage if you have it?" "We certainly do Sir. I am sure you are aware although a French wine, Alsace does border Germany and so does produce a crisp dry white wine" "Yes, of course, that will be fine" "Here are your menus for you to look at, I will be back shortly to take your orders". The lady scurried off to the bar.

"It's not a big menu and they don't do specials Joan, but Jenny Fenney, from work, comes here a lot so it must be good" "I have already seen what I am having Liam, what about you?" "Funnily enough I have too". The lady arrived back and poured a glass of wine for Liam to try. "Excellent thank you" "Would you like to order or would you like a while longer?"

"We're both ready to order, thank you" "Ok Madam, what would you like?" "Yes, could I have the Seasoned Scallops with Seared Roe to start, followed by Turbot with Mussels and chives and the medley of garden vegetables please?" "Certainly, and for you Sir?" "I'll have Lamb Sweetbread with Asparagus and fermented Turnip, followed by Aged Aberdeen Angus tips, with bone Marrow Oyster Leaf and Lovage mushrooms with Sauté potatoes please".

They had a most enjoyable night, Liam was hanging on every word this beautiful woman spoke. They never mentioned the dreams, it was like they knew everything now and they were happy.

New Year's Eve arrived and the big day for Liam. While Joan was showering ready for a night in York, Liam checked he had the engagement ring. He had really pushed the boat out, in his opinion the most beautiful girl he had ever met, deserved the most beautiful ring. The ring he had purchased had two one carat diamonds with a one carat emerald sat in the centre. He had had it made especially, from a picture of his great grandmother's ring. Who apparently came from a well to do family but was ostracised when she met her husband, Liam's Granddad. Her family said she had married below her station and she was immediately cut out of the family estate by her father.

Joan looked beautiful, she was dressed in a black dress with a square sculpted neck line, the dress length was just above her knees. She had black and white Jimmy Choo shoes and she complemented the dress with a string of small pearls.

"Wow, you look fabulous Joan" "All for you my dear handsome man". They walked hand in hand along the river. "Would you mind if we just went inside York Minster? I always like to go in there when I visit York" "Of course I don't. I would love to, it looks so regal". The Minster was lit up like a bright, shining beacon; people from all over the City were drawn to this magnificent building.

"Liam will you take my picture before we go in?" Liam looked through the lens on Joan's iPhone; he had to shake his head clear. Through the lens he could see Shona in a wedding dress not Joan!! He took the picture and showed it to Joan. "Let me look Liam". She was pleased, but again what was happening? It was like Shona knew Liam was going to ask Joan to marry him he thought. They entered the Minster. "This is taking my breath away Liam, it is so beautiful and so peaceful".

I could not tell Joan that I felt cold all over. It was as if I was stood naked in a freezer room. I felt like something was trying to suck my happiness out of me. We carried on down to the front and I asked Joan to enter in to one of the pews. "Joan I want to ask you something", I dropped on one knee and produced the ring, "Will you marry me my darling?" There was a silence and tears began to roll down Joan's beautiful face. "Yes, yes, of course I will". They kissed. Then a fire alarm sounded and they were ushered out of the Minster by one of the clergy. "Never in my sixty six years have I ever known an evacuation situation, even when I was a ten year old choir boy" said the elderly gentleman.

It was quite cold outside, but not as cold as I had felt in the Minster. New Year's Revellers were everywhere, even some dressed as buccaneers. That spooked me somewhat. We visited a few bars and watched the midnight fireworks from the balcony of the hotel. Joan was happy with her ring and I am sure my great grandmother would have been looking down on us with a smile on her face. "I feel shattered Joan, I think I am going to get in bed" "Well I am coming with you Mr Egan, seeing that I am officially to be Mrs Egan". They fell into each other's arms and were soon asleep. It had been a long day and since the feeling I had in the Minster, I felt drained.

My dreams came to me almost immediately. I was sat on the wrap-round porch of Tree Cliff House. Shona was sewing; I sat watching my beautiful lady. How fortunes had changed for all of us. I could see Jankay and Labron laughing in the walled garden, they seemed so happy it pleasured my heart so much. I decided to tell Shona of my plans to marry her. I built up the courage and with a deep breath I blurted it out. "Will you marry me fair lady" Shona looked at me and for a second I thought she was going to say no.

"Before I answer you Cabhan, I also have some news. I am with child so if you still want me as your wife, I will gladly accept"

I sat speechless maybe after all the terrible things that had happened to me in my life it was all meant to be. I met my wife who I admire, respect and love with every part of my being and now I am to be a father to a beautiful child. I hugged and kissed Shona and shouted to Jankay and Labron to come to the house. I got all the maids together and everyone that worked at Tree Cliff House.

Everyone stood together on the lawn whilst I stood on the porch steps with Shona. "Today I have an announcement which I want to share with you all my good friends. Shona and I are to be married and Shona is also with child" Everyone cheered it was like a party, the whole atmosphere was one of happiness and joy.

We partied until the early hours of the next day. I told Shona I was going into

Timmid to see the priest and we would get married the following day. I instructed the cooks to make a banquet fit for a king, no expense spared, and I asked Jankay to organise the whole of Clew Bay to be present at Tree Cliff House.

I rode into Timmid to see the preacher, I didn't mention Shona was with child for fear of damnation from the preacher. He agreed to marry us in the little chapel in the grounds of Tree Cliff House. When I arrived back to the house, bunting had been festooned everywhere, even on the approach to the chapel. Pigs were being slowly roasted on a spit, by Mrs McGuire and her team of cooks, the night smelt of food.

The preacher said the wedding would take place at 10.30am the following morning. Neither Shona nor I could sleep that night, after all we had done to just be together, this was our wish come true. I lay with one arm round her and one hand resting on her tummy and our baby.

LOOKING FOR SHONA

I woke up with a start, I was sweating profusely. "Liam are you ok? Can't you sleep? It's only 3.30am" "Oh sorry Joan, I must have had a bad dream" "Hope it wasn't about us" "I don't think so, I can't remember". All the time Liam was talking to Joan he was thinking about the wedding to Shona, but he couldn't say that to Joan, they had their own wedding to plan and he didn't want Joan to feel second best.

With the holidays now over and Liam back at work, things settled down. There had been no more dreams and the wedding plans were going well. The venue Joan chose was Gilkin Hall, a magnificent Tudor Hall that specialised in weddings. With two weeks to go the Saturday had been put aside for the stag weekend. Jamie was disappointed that Vegas was knocked back, but he arranged a day at the races, then they were flying to Dublin for two nights. Jamie, of course, went over the top. He had arranged a stretch limo for the journey to the races. Liam's brother and his mate had arrived along with Jamie, Stan and his mate Jerry or Jerry Berry has Jamie had nicknamed

243

him, that left just one seat, which Ian Ludlow was occupying.

They had only been left ten minutes or so, when the three bottles of Champagne that came with the hire of the limo, had already been consumed. The boys started singing "We want more beer, we want more beer" "Ok you rowdy lot, there is a Tesco's round the next corner, you can nip in there". Jamie, being the poser he was, told all the lads to stick their sunglasses on. They were all wearing suits and he made the driver pull up right outside the main doors, so all the girls on the cash outs could see them. "They will think we are some high paid footballers".

Armed with ten bottles of champagne and a bottle of Chivas Regal, they got back in the limo. "Drive on my good man and don't spare the horses" Jamie shouted from the back. "You are a prat Jamie, but I love you" and Liam rubbed his knuckles across Jamie's carefully groomed hair. They arrived at Haydock Park in a state that can only be described as dishevelled. "You got any tips Jerry Berry?" "Yeah don't dunk your Rich Tea biscuit in your tea for too long". Everyone laughed. They were studying the bookies when Liam's mobile rang. "Hey sweetheart you ok? Although I'm not sure you will be when I tell you something" "What's the matter?" "I have just done a pregnancy test and its positive Liam" said Joan. Liam let out a cry of joy "Whoooo, oh babe that's fantastic news" "I didn't know if I should wait to tell you, but I was so excited I wanted to share it with you now. Listen have a lovely few days, guess I won't be drinking on my hen night tonight. You men get all the best perks" and she laughed, "I love you" "I love you too Joan", said Liam.

"Blimey she can't leave you alone boy" teased Jamie. "I'm going to be a dad" said a stunned Liam. "Really? Oh my God that's great news mate" "Hey you lot hear this lads, we have a new daddy out with us today". All the lads were congratulating Liam.

"Right, now let's get down to some serious stuff, like caning these bookies" said Jamie. Nobody won until the fifth race. "Hey Liam look at this, Baby Paddy, you got to go big on that". Jerry suggested they all stick a hundred quid on it. Jamie collected the money. "Seven hundred quid lads, are we going each way or on the nose?". Everyone other than Ian wanted on the nose. "Ok decision made, seven hundred pound to win on Baby Paddy". They checked the bookies, Jerry Berry seemed to understand horses so he found the best price. "Bloody Hell lads, I think it's a Skegness donkey it's forty to one" "So what will we win if it comes in Jerry Berry?" "Two thousand and eight hundred quid between us" answered Jerry.

Let's go down to the rails and watch the finish. There were five horses over three miles. First to show was Eagle King followed closely by Brian Bump then came Baby Paddy, Silk Coat and the favourite Magic Kev. After two mile there was nothing to choose other than Baby Paddy was now last. With four fences to jump Eagle King up ended his rider and the horse tampered with Brian Bump and brought that horse down. With three fences to go Eagle King was leading, followed by the favourite Magic Kev and poor old Baby Paddy was a good three lengths behind and looking like his jockey might pull him up. At the final fence Magic Kev fell. "Should have done it each way, I told you!" "Ah shut up Ian, there were only five in it and the bookies weren't accepting each way". Suddenly there was big gasp from the crowd. The commentator remarked "I have never seen anything like this Eagle King has stopped running and thrown his jockey off. The only horse left in the running is Baby Paddy who is yet to jump the last. If he gets over this, he will win in this very strange race". Baby Paddy approached the last and with one last effort, he blundered through the fence but was ok and finished to the amazement of the crowd.

Jerry Berry kissed the ticket, "Come on you beauty!", he cried. "Oh wow, that was exciting Liam" "Must be your lucky day mate". Liam was beaming with joy. Of course the day carried on with the bookies winning all the other races but it didn't matter they had a sizeable win. It was now back to the hotel, a night in Liverpool then the flight to Dublin.

The following morning they all looked pretty ill at breakfast, except Jamie who said he felt good, as he tucked in to a man-sized fry up. "I can't sit with you Jamie, just watching you with that runny egg is making me feel sick" "Ha, ha should have done what I did Liam, never drank from the grape and the grain" "What do you mean?" "Well if you'd have watched, I stuck with everything made from the grape, where as you lot drank drinks from the grape and the grain, not good my son, not good". Jamie offered Liam a piece of egg on his fork, Liam disappeared to the toilet for almost twenty minutes, there were three others in there as well, Liam's brother and his mate and Jerry Berry, all blaming Stan for feeling so unwell. "Did you see how many flaming Sambuca's Stan could drink? We had five each and he must have had another three, and he looks fit as a butchers dog this morning".

Jamie rounded them all up and they were soon on their way to Dublin. Once landed and through customs Jamie instructed the taxi driver to the hotel. "Laflin boutique Hotel, please" "Very plush Jamie, you have done us proud mate". "It looked good on the website", he replied. A pretty receptionist booked them in, with Jamie telling Stan to put his tongue back as he drooled over her.

Liam had been a bit apprehensive about Ireland for his stag weekend, but didn't want to appear to be ruining the day. He could not remember Dublin and didn't have any Déjà Vu moments so that was good. The boys were out from 1.00pm finally getting back into the hotel at 2.20am the following morning. Luckily Liam had his own room everyone else was sharing.

He undressed and got into a lovely comfy bed and was soon asleep, only now the dreams had started again.

It was the morning of the wedding, Jankay was to be my best man and how splendid

he looked, he was smiling his biggest
smile. "Who would have thought my good
friend, on that very first day I met you,
that one day we would be stood in a
church together and you waiting for your
beautiful bride?" "I know Jankay so much
has happened, so much bad stuff, such as
Oday and Lomo, but so much good with
the beautiful lives we now have".

The church was full of the estate workers,
all the oak pews had been decorated with
flowers. The church was festooned with
beautiful flowers everywhere.

The moment had come, my wife to be
walked down the aisle chaperoned by
Labron, he also had the biggest infectious
smile. Mr Ross the preacher was
somewhat taken aback when Shona lifted
her veil to reveal her beautiful black skin.
With a clearing of his throat he carried on.
His final words "I now pronounce ye man
and wife", were the words I never thought
I would hear in the darkest moments of
our lives. With those words the
celebrations began, they would carry on

for another two days before things started to get back to normal.

It was eight months later as I returned from a business trip, to be met by one of the maids. "Quickly Sir, Miss Shona is about to give birth". I ran up the winding oak stair case with every emotion running through my veins. I just got to the bedroom when little Lomo Oday came into this world. We had decided to call him or her after our two friends who gave their lives so that this little person could have a life.

Now our life was complete, Shona was tired but so pleased I got back in time to see our son born. This was a special day in our lives and I told Shona that as I kissed her gently on the cheek.

The next thing I knew I was waking up under some bright lights. "Joan what are you doing here, what happened?" "They found you in the hotel room; they think you had another seizure" "Where am I?" "We are still in Dublin, in St Patrick's Hospital, you have been in a coma for almost a month. If you feel well enough, we are to marry in two weeks' time. I haven't cancelled anything, I was praying you were going to be ok" "I feel fine Joan" "Well let's see what the doctors say, they will be doing their rounds in a few minutes".

"Mr Egan, James Fullness, I have been looking after you. You have your friends to thank that you are here today, they found you and got you here. I believe by your records this is the second time this has happened. Is that correct?". "Yes it is" "Ok Mr Egan, I need to explain what exactly your brain is going through. The seizure's that you have had experienced, the first one and this one, are not uncommon but the likely hood of you having more as time goes on is now increased, because of the second one. My other concern is that you appear to go into a coma for a long period of time, we have scanned your brain and we can't find anything that could be attributed to the comas".

"What exactly is it Doctor?" asked Liam. "You are getting electrical activity, this is caused by a complex chemical change that occurs in your nerve cells. Something is triggering these seizures, I have notes from your previous experience and it appears either by coincidence or cause, you were in Ireland when you had your last seizure. Is there anything you can tell us, that you think may have triggered this problem? Are you under an enormous amount of stress etc? I will state seizures are not a disease in themselves. Instead they are a symptom of many disorders that can affect the brain. Some seizures can be hardly noticed, yet some can be totally disabling. You Mr Egan appear to have the latter. I am afraid to tell you this, but you could go onto develop full blown epilepsy, therefore you need to see your own doctor on your return. He will possibly subscribe a suitable medication, if not certainly some kind of monitoring program. I hope I have explained your condition in a manner you understand, and if your GP has any further questions, he can contact me directly. You are free to leave the hospital tomorrow morning Mr

Egan. Good day". "Thank you" Liam replied and the specialist left the room.

"Blimey Joan, do you still want to marry me?" "Of course why wouldn't I?" Liam was fine when they left Dublin and the wedding went ahead as planned. Joan had to do all of the organising herself, most of it whilst Liam was in a coma.

The big day arrived, Jamie and Liam called for a drink at the Lamb Inn, just a short walk to the church in the lovely village of Lower Slowly, near Knutsford in Cheshire. Joan had chosen this church as she had been christened there; she didn't know why her mother had never said.

Jamie and Liam ordered a drink with the landlord at the Lamb. He was a jovial fellow cracking jokes. "So where are you lads from, are you off to a wedding?" "Yes it's mine". "What time are you doing that stupid thing to yourself?" and he laughed. "1.15pm". Jamie looked at Liam and Liam kicked Jamie, they both knew it was at 2.45pm. "Well if you have any sense you won't bother going. I have been married twice and it's cost me a bloody fortune". For the next hour the landlord bombarded Liam with reason's not to get married.

At 1.00pm Jamie ordered two more glass of scotch. The landlord, thinking that Liam had actually taken his advice, started to go back on what he'd said about not getting married. "Don't think you will have time for another drink". Liam spoke up. "I was just saying to Jamie, you talk a lot of sense, so you are right I'm not getting married you made my mind up. Thank you for that"

"Hey lad, take no notice of me, Freda and I have been married thirty seven years we have three kids and seven lovely grandchildren. I was only joking, it was best thing I ever did marrying my Freda". Liam and Jamie carried on with the fun they were having. It got to 1.20pm and the landlord was in panic, so he shouted his wife down. "Just tell this young man how long we have been married" "Too bloody long!!" Jamie jumped on that straight away, "See there is your answer, now let's have more scotch and celebrate my mate's close shave". The landlord then had a go at Freda and when she understood what had happened she started back tracking. Liam couldn't help himself anymore. "It's a joke, I won't be married until 2.45pm" he laughed. "Bloody hell lad, I was sweating there." "Well seeing that we had some fun, you and Freda are very welcome at the night do, if you can make it?" "Well that's very nice of you lad, but Saturday night is our busiest but you have this scotch on me and trust me I have learned my lesson".

They left the little pub at 2.20pm and took the short walk to the church. "I am feeling nervous Jamie" "You will be fine, you are lucky man Mr Egan. She is a lovely girl and so pretty" "Well thanks Jamie, I have to agree". They had been stood at the front for fifteen minutes when the organist struck up the wedding march. Liam could feel the butterflies in his tummy. Joan finally arrived at the altar and lifted her veil. She looked beautiful; her wedding dress was fitted with it just off her shoulders. She had three bridesmaids. They were the girls she had been at the club with on the first night she met Liam.

The bridesmaids were all in a dark purple, which complemented the brides dress. The vicar went through the service. Liam fluffed his line saying 'cherish and love' instead of 'love and cherish', but other than that it all went well. Those magic words were spoken by the vicar. "You may now kiss the bride"
Liam leaned forward, but suddenly had a flash back to Cabhan and Shona's wedding from his dreams. "Are you ok Liam?" He recomposed himself and put right the situation. "Sorry Joan, how could I not be alright? I have the most beautiful girl in the world as my wife".

Back at the hotel the little photographer was busying himself organising the families. With wives, shouting their husbands from the bar and kids running round playing and mothers telling them 'to get up off the grass or they would ruin their trousers and dresses and did they know how much these things cost?' the photographer was kept busy.

"You ok mate? I thought for a minute you weren't going to kiss poor Joan." "I had a flashback mate. If anything happens, don't forget were my diary is will you?". "Stop being soft, it's your wedding day." "I know, but I sense all these things have a meaning Jamie." "Of course I will read your diary, now let's bloody get on with the best day of your life." 'It's alright for Jamie to say that', he thought but the truth he was feeling was, he wanted to be with Shona in the dream.

The photographer was very persistent, "Button you coats up lads, no beer belly's hanging out too ruin the wedding shots". After almost one and half hours the wedding photography was done. Now it was time for the speeches.

First up was a friend of Joan, because her father had died many years before.

"First of all could I say how honoured I am to have been asked by Joan to give her away today. Joan is a special, talented girl and I know I speak for all the family when I say 'welcome to the family Liam'. I would also like to thank you all, because I know some of you have travelled a long way to be here to share Joan and Liam's special day. Finally, I would like you all to raise your glasses and share with me our best wishes for a happy and contented life for the happy couple. Thank you"

Much clinking of champagne flutes could be heard, and then a couple of the lads were shouting for Jamie to get up. Stan who was being the toastmaster shouted for order. "Next to speak is the groom". Liam stood up.

Liam thanked Philip for all he had done for Joan. "I would also like to thank the beautiful bridesmaids and best friends to Joan" and Liam passed across a small box for each girl containing a cross on a necklace.

"I'm not very good at this, so it's time for Jamie to take centre stage". Millie laughed as she looked at Liam.

"Order!" and Jamie clinked his glass with his spoon. "For those of you that don't know me, I'm Jamie and have been a close friend of Liam's for many years, ever since we came to work together. In that time I have been a partner in crime on many occasions and in the quieter moments a confidante for Liam, someone to whom he can tell anything - which provides me with ample material for my speech this afternoon".

"Now I did ask for a microphone, but was told there wasn't one available. So if you can't hear me at the back, the silence from the people at the front should re-assure you that you are not missing out on anything. I guess being best man is like having sex with Jenny, nobody wants to do it, but it is an honour". The line didn't go down to well as there were three Jenny's in the room. "Now I realise that you all must think I am talking about a Jenny in the room, well you are wrong, take a look three better looking girls you could not wish to meet". Liam covered his mouth with his hand and said "You saved yourself there old lad"

"My next piece of advice is just for you Liam"

"Married life can be compared to football. So be fully committed every week and make sure you score at least once every weekend. Make sure you change ends at half time. Don't put your tackle in too hard or you might injure yourself. However, Joan assures me that playing away from home will result in a serious injury and will immediately place you on the transfer list. That got a round of applause. Tell you what, you lot are hard work, but don't worry I have more"

"As with all best man/groom relationships, there are the stories I'm not allowed to tell. Like the time myself and Liam ended up in the casualty department after one Saturday night out. However if you see me at the bar later, I may be persuaded to reveal all. Anyway all joking aside, please raise your glasses to the bridesmaids and to Laura the chief bridesmaid, who I believe I have to have a dance with. Not that it's a hardship just that Millie my wife will be throwing the daggers, won't you my lovely?" Millie just smiled. "Of course, well done to the best man, whoever he is what a suave debonair guy he is" and everyone laughed. "Big thanks to the ushers for staying sober and turning up at the right church, which was always going to be a worry with those lads. Finally please raises your glasses with me to toast two lovely people, who I am sure will have many a long years together in happiness and love. Liam and Joan, ladies and gentlemen". The guest's all raised their glasses and cheered.

The day was a total success and before Liam and Joan went down for the evening bash, Joan asked Liam to sit down. "Wow this looks serious already Joan, are you stopping my Saturday golf with Jamie?" "Don't be daft. It's just when I did the pregnancy test, when you were on the stags do, that morning when I told you I was pregnant you made me feel so special and I love you so much Mr Egan". "I can't begin to tell you what those magic words meant to me Joan" "Oh that is such a relief; I was hoping you would not be mad at me" "Mad at you? I am over the moon" "I don't want to tell anyone yet Liam, until I am showing. I think its bad luck". "Of course I understand, I am so happy Joan". Luckily Liam didn't realise all the lads on the stag do knew, because he had been so excited he'd told them. Joan shed a small tear. "I love you Egan" "I love you too Mrs Egan" and they both smiled. "Come on we best get downstairs to the guests".

The DJ saw them both walking down the stairs so he put the most Beautiful Girl in the World on the turntable everyone was clapping.

"Ok everyone, now we have our beautiful couple back the song they have chosen for the first dance is "Islands in the Stream" by the great Dolly Parton and Kenny Rogers please make a circle round the perimeter of the dance floor".

As they danced Joan said "Maybe we should have had Baby Jane!!" "You are not wrong there sweetheart" as he twirled Joan round, much to the delight of the on looking guests. They had decided not to honeymoon as Joan had to go to Ethiopia with work two days later.

The following morning they met the guests for breakfast and the usual banter from Stan and the lads ensued. "Long night was it?" "Very funny Stan" "Would not have been very long if the rumours are correct hey Liam?" "My we are on form this morning Trenchey". "Only joking mate". After the breakfast Liam paid the bill for the wedding and the rooms. They both waved off their respective families and headed back to London. Joan lay on Liam's arm while he drove, nuzzling his neck, much to his delight.

As they arrived at the flat Liam's phone went. "Hi mate, are you up for a round of golf at 3.00pm with me and Stan?" "Well hardly bud; I have only just got married". "Go Liam", said Joan "I will be fine, I have to get things ready for my trip so no big deal" "Blimey you are some woman Mrs Egan, what a lucky guy I am".

LOOKING FOR SHONA

Liam arrived at Devonshire Golf Club just before 3.00pm and was parking the car as Stan and Jamie arrived. "Bloody hell mate, that is some woman you have there, I don't think Millie would have been as understanding on the first day after getting hitched".

"Yeah I am a lucky man." "You certainly are." "Right, what are we playing for? A tenner a hole and the one who wins the least tenners, buys a meal and the beers". "Yeah good with me, but so you don't think I am tight, I am only stopping for one for obvious reasons". "Heard that one before Liam" and Stan and Jamie laughed.

The Devonshire course had been laid by one of the Dukes of Devonshire around 1902. It had been considered for the Open a few times. The scenery was just outstanding, the greens were so lush they almost looked artificial or as if they had been painted. The first hole was a par four, over a lake. Jamie hit a screamer just a hundred yards from the green. Next up Stan cleared the lake but his ball rolled into a bunker. By now Liam was giving it large "Do you lads want to pay me now and we can just go to the bar?" "Just wait a minute Rory McIlroy, hasn't tee'd off yet" Liam remarked as he placed the ball on his pin. With one almighty whack his ball went high in the air then plopped smack in the middle of the lake, damn, he thought then he tried again this time almost the same thing happened. By now Stan and Jamie were rolling about laughing. "Throw it over Liam we don't mind" "Bollocks you two" he retorted.

As Liam swung he suddenly collapsed. Jamie and Stan had started walking over bridge to get to the lake on the other side where their balls lay. Jamie turned to see if Liam had hit his second shot. "Stan quick, Liam is lying on the ground!! Call an ambulance" Jamie was first there, Liam was incoherent. "Liam, Liam, come on mate hang on, please mate hang on we are getting help".

The ambulance arrived and the Paramedics tended to Liam. "I'm going with him, phone Joan and Millie tell them

we will be at Darlow General Hospital."
"Ok mate I will see you there in a bit".

Liam was now was back in his dream with
Shona, at her bedside looking at his newly
born son, Lomo Oday. He was beautiful
only lightly skinned with big dark brown
eyes and already curly black hair. "He is a
fine boy my darling, you have made me
very proud" and he smiled.

Over the coming years life was idyllic for
Cabhan and Shona. The head gardener
sadly passed away, but by then Jankay
being the proud man he was, took up his
post. Jankay had bought a small crofting
cottage and had married Aoi. They had
two little girls Ramkin and Sulu.
Everything seemed perfect.

Ireland was going through tough times but
Cabhan had investments all over and was
now very rich, so it wasn't affecting him,
his staff or friends. Once a week he would
go into Clew Bay to give fresh fruit and
vegetables to the poor families and
nobody in Clew Bay had to pay rent to
him. Cabhan and Shona were loved and

respected in the community. They did this as a thank you for how their lives had turned out.

It was Christmas 1649 when word came to Cabhan that Cromwell's soldiers were attacking Ireland and seizing land under the pretense of revenge for the 1641 uprising. Irish land owners were being thrown off their land and being forced west. Cabhan knew this wasn't good and worst to come, was he had been an ally of the King so he knew they would know of him.

That Christmas was a massive strain on Cabhan's family, every day over the Christmas period word was coming back that farmers were being put off their land.

It was the night of February 12th a cold wet miserable night. Cabhan was playing with Lomo Oday in front of the fire. Shona was sat sewing. There was a loud banging on the door. "Just a second son, let me see who that is". Cabhan lowered Lomo Oday off his back and walked down the hallway into the magnificent greeting area of the house. The door was being violently banged on. "Alright, alright I'm coming". Cabhan opened the door he was met by the sight of his neighbour, Mr Rashleigh. There was blood dripping from a wound to his arm. "Quickly Shona, get me some hot water and bandages". Rashleigh was exhausted and his wound was becoming infected. Cabhan carried him to one of the guest rooms and laid him on the bed and dressed his wounds he had a deep cut to his upper arm.

"Cabhan you have to get your family out of here, the roundheads are coming. I was at one of your farms in Doolinar; my sister is married to Charles Macken. The roundheads came and took your farm in the name of England and Cromwell Lord Protector. My sister protested and was slain in front of our very eyes. Charles was taken. I slipped out the back way as all this was happening, but met a soldier as I climbed on my horse. He drew his sword and slashed my arm, but I managed to get away. They didn't follow me they were too busy raping and pillaging the family". "But Doolinar is some two

269

hundred miles away. How the hell have you managed to get here?" "I stopped at as many farms as I could on the way, trying to warn them. At the last farm as I left, I slipped off my horse and caught my arm which made the wound worse".

Cabhan finished dressing the wound and asked the house maid to give Mr Rashleigh some Irish stew, bread and whisky so that he may sleep. Shona asked Cabhan what were they to do.

"Get some clothes and provisions take Lomo Oday, Aoi and her children and the servants with you, tell Jankay and Labron to come to the house. Take plenty of provisions down into the rock cave under the cliffs at Clew Bay and wait for me there I will come for you".

I ordered one of the man servants to get all the guns, which meant there were eight of us. "Cabhan how long will it take for the boat to be ready?" "I am guessing by dawn tomorrow with a bit of luck". "We can't fight these people, we have to find a new home for all of us" "I have money we

270

can take and once we have settled, maybe somewhere off Scotland, then I can go and get my affairs in order. We just need to try and hold them while everybody gets on board the ship, so we can leave".

Suddenly Rashleigh appeared at the top of the stairs with a gun. "You ok Mr Rashleigh?" Rashleigh fired his gun, it just missed Jankay. "What the hell are you doing?" "You are all stupid, I work for Oliver Cromwell, The Lord Protector, and by the power invested in me I claim this house and your lands. Do not resist me the house is surrounded. You will not be harmed if you leave peacefully and sign this declaration". Cabhan was so angry, he had invited this man into his house, fed and tended his wounds and all the time he was plotting to take my livelihood away from me, my friends and family.

Cabhan bolted up the stairs before Rashleigh could reload, he grabbed him round the neck and threw him over the banister rail. Rashleigh hit the floor with a thud and died immediately. Next another shot was fired from outside. They could hear soldiers trying to get in, eventually the soldiers in their leather tunics and high leather boots and metal helmet with a guard, appeared. They had muskets in hand with some having pikes to do battle. Cromwell's army had broken into the house and in the hallway fighting was fierce, luckily there were only maybe a dozen men. By the time it was over the hallway was full of musket smoke and blood was everywhere from the dead. Jankay and Cabhan started looking through the dead bodies and only they had survived. Labron had fallen his head had been severed by a soldiers Pike. Jankay held him, clearly shaken by the brutality of the battle.

Jankay we don't have a lot of time, we need to go and help get the ship sorted to sail. We all need to load up the carts and take as much provision as can muster down to the ship.

Everybody did as Cabhan instructed, with the ship ready Cabhan and Jankay went back up the cliff face to the cave for everyone. Just as they started to leave more of the New Model Army had arrived intent on revenge. Shona was holding Lomo Oday's hand as they tried to get down to Cabhan. The first to fall was Aoi, she fell forward and fell off the rock face. Jankay was like a madman and would not be restrained by Cabhan. The emergence of Cabhan, helped some of the others get down the hill side to him. "Get on the ship all of you, I have to help Jankay". Shona grabbed Cabhan's arm "I love you my darling" Cabhan looked at her, smiled and ran back up the cliff side. By now Jankay was fighting off three soldiers.

Cabhan killed the first soldier with one blow but he was too late to save Jankay his head was partially severed by the soldiers Pike. Cabhan swung round and managed hit one of the two remaining soldiers with a Pike that was lay on the ground. Finally the third soldier was clearly now frightened and Cabhan threw him off the cliff face.

"Goodbye my friend, I have no time to bury you if I am to save the others and he patted Jankay's body as he scrambled down the Cliff face. Remembering that before the soldiers broke in the house, Jankay said he had a boy back on St Lucia who he had never seen. 'That boy will never know that brilliant man' he thought.

Just as they were about to lift anchor Liam's body went into an uncontrollable shake. Joan, who had hardly left his side, in the years Liam, had been in a coma, shouted for help,. Nurses and doctors appeared and pushed Joan to the outside. "Come on love, he is in good hands" the kindly nurse said.

Joan was shaking. Almost an hour had gone by when Joan looked at the clock it was 3.30am. The Doctor, a Mr Sling, came from behind the drawn curtains towards Joan. "Mrs Egan, your husband has come out of his coma, he will need rest but he is talking with no obvious side effects. We will do a brain scan tomorrow, but if you don't mind I don't want him to have lots of visitors, we need to try and understand what is triggering these effects on your husband's brain" "Ok Sir, I understand". Joan put her head round the curtains to look at Liam and it was as if he had woken from a dream he seemed perfectly fine, other than he had lost so much of his life.

"What can you remember Liam?" "I can remember we got married and I remember playing golf" and Liam laughed "They are the last things I remember" "You have a daughter Liam, I named her Jane. Remember our wedding night when I told you I was pregnant and then at our first dance we said we should have asked for 'Baby Jane'? Well because you weren't there to decide with me, I chose Jane Shona Egan" "They are pretty names, where did you get Shona from?" Liam was now not appearing to remember his dreams, so maybe that was a good thing.

The doctors looked at everything and still could find no reason for Liam's seizures. The good thing was, the dreams had stopped and life for the next ten years was normal.

It was the eve of Jane's birthday and she asked if it was ok to go to a club in town with her friends to celebrate her birthday the following evening. Liam reluctantly agreed, she was the apple of her daddy's eye and he was very protective of her. "You have to let her make her own mistakes now Liam" "I know Joan, but I lost all those years when she was growing up" "I know darling. Shall we ask Millie and Jamie over tomorrow night, it might take your mind off it all?" "Sounds like a good idea those two have been having it rough with Millie's parents passing away, both within a year of each other. Jamie has had a bad back and some days can hardly move. I think that's a great idea". Jane was happy Liam was letting her have some freedom, so the night ended with a nice atmosphere.

Joan and Liam went to bed and after all these years they still had a passion which hadn't been dimmed with the passing of time.

Once asleep, Liam for the first time in ten years had his dream start again.

He was lifting anchor on the ship, for some reason Cabhan's life hadn't moved on like Liam's had. With most of the men folk dead the soldiers were soon over-running the boat. They brutally murdered the servants and Cabhan's Lomo Oday, his son, and then they made Cabhan watch while they raped Shona repeatedly. The poor girl was a mess, all her clothes were ripped. Cabhan was shackled and could do nothing, she cried "Help me Cabhan, please help me". One of the soldiers started taunting Cabhan. "Bog Arab, your little lady is serving a need of the soldiers is that ok with you?" "You bastard, let me out of these chains and I will kill you with my bare hands."

"I tell you what I will do, you can fight my two best soldiers, they will have knives and you can use your bare hands and if you win we will stop raping her. If my soldiers win, then we will throw her overboard for the fish, is that a deal?" Cabhan had no choice. "Release the Bog Arab, Suffolk and Jenkins, dispose of this low life" Cabhan fought valiantly killing Suffolk. Cabhan by now was exhausted and cut in many places on his body. All the soldiers were laughing, his poor Shona was crying for her husband and their dead son. With every breath he had and every ounce of strength, Cabhan pulled Jenkins to the floor. He was just about to break his neck when the Captain laid his sword across Cabhan's neck. "You lose my friend" he said and he nodded to the other two soldiers who then threw Shona over board, you could hear her scream as she hit the rocks below.

"Now Bog Arab, your turn Jenkins, run this lowlife through and throw him over board to be with his wife and child" Jenkins thrust his sword across Cabhan's chest and he fell to the deck. Three soldiers then through his body over board.

Liam woke up sweating; "Darling are you ok?" they both glanced at the clock again 3.30am. Liam explained what had happened. "Oh my darling, sadly this maybe the end of this" "I hope so Joan." "Come on, try and get some sleep." "No, I think I will get a coffee and write the rest of the dream in my diary" "Well don't stress yourself out Liam, I don't want you poorly again." "I won't darling" and Liam headed for the kitchen. The sun was rising as he finished the diary, he wrapped it in some brown paper and wrote 'for my best friend Jamie thank you for your support I love you as much as I loved Jankay' and he added two exclamation marks.

It was now 9.30am and both Joan and Jane were up and about. "Happy Birthday my Princess" he said to his daughter "Thank you dad, and thank you for trusting me tonight." "Just be careful Princess, it's a tough old world out there and there is always somebody ready to hurt you." "I will dad thank you for my necklace, I love it." "Good Princess, treasure it for the rest of your life".

"So what is the plan today?" asked Jane. "Well me and Dad are going into town to do some shopping, Aunty Millie and Uncle Jamie are coming over for a meal tonight." "That's nice mum, Uncle Jamie is such a nutter." "Always been the same love, he was like that when I first met your Dad, he was dancing in a club on his own." "Really, how crazy is that?" "What are you up to?" "Mira is coming round and we are going to roller world with mates from school, then we are out tonight to a club for my first legal drink." "Well just be careful." "Will do Mum, won't see you until tomorrow I am getting changed at Mira's." "Here is twenty pounds, you make sure you get a taxi home Princess." Said Liam "Will do Dad" replied Jane.

"Come on then Liam, let's get down the high street before all the best cuts of meat are gone." "I'm coming dear." "Cut the sarcasm Egan" and Joan laughed. Even after all these years they were clearly very much in love as they walked down the high street hand in hand. "Look at those beautiful vegetables Liam." "What are you going to make Joan?" "I thought Moroccan lamb would be good." "Sounds perfect to me." Liam paid for the vegetables, as they left the shop Joan tripped and the bag of vegetables rolled everywhere. Joan leaned forward and bent down to pick up the cabbage that had rolled into the road. She hadn't seen the bus, but Liam had, he pushed her out of the way but the bus hit Liam killing him instantly. The bus driver visibly shaken was trying to explain that there was nothing he could do. The Saturday shoppers gathered round Liam's body, they called the police and an ambulance but he was dead on arrival at the hospital.

Joan was in a state of shock as she left the hospital with Jamie, Millie and Jane. "How could this happen on my birthday mum" sobbed Jane. Once back in the flat Jamie made everyone a strong tea with some sugar in for the shock. Millie noticed the brown paper parcel on the table. "What's that Joan?" "I think it's some kind of diary that Liam wanted Jamie to have. Take it, he must have wanted you to have it Jamie." They sat sipping tea in almost absolute silence. There was a knock on the door Jamie went to answer it two police officers one man and a women had come to take Joan's statement. "We are very sorry for your loss Madam, but we have to take a statement to see if there are any unusual circumstances, we won't keep you long." Joan nodded. "You are Mr Egan's wife,

Joan Egan, is that correct?" Joan nodded again, "If you could run through what happened when the 330 bus to Islington hit Mr Egan. Ironically at 3.30pm today." Joan started to explain in between wiping the tears from her eyes,

After about twenty minutes the officers thanked Joan for her statement and left the flat. "Do you want us to stay with you tonight Joan?" "No there is no need honestly." "We would feel better if you would, let us look after you" "Well if you are sure you don't mind Millie thank you." Joan turned to Jane. "Go and enjoy your evening your dad would have wanted that". "How can I enjoy my night when my dad died today?" "Your dad only went to heaven today sweetheart and you know how regimented he was about things and he promised when you were eighteen you could go to a club so please do it for me and dad." "Ok if you put it like that mum." "Get ready and I will run over to your mates Jane" "Thank you Uncle Jamie." "Thanks Jamie" "No problem Joan, me and Millie love her, like we were

her parents, she has made a lovely girl."
"Thank you." replied Joan

Jamie took Jane to her mates and gave her a fifty pound note. "Have a drink for me and your dad." "Thank you Uncle Jamie, you are so kind, dad loved you like a brother."

On the way back Jamie decided to stop and have a drink in his and Liam's favourite boozer, he got his pint of Timothy Taylor's Landlord bitter then sat in the corner and started to read the diary Liam had left him. He hadn't realized how much that crazy night on January 12ᵗʰ all those years ago had affected Liam. The more he read the more he wanted to read. After almost two hours his phone rang, which made him jump. "Where are you Jamie?" "Oh I am sorry, I stopped for a drink on the way back in the pub me and Liam loved and just lost track of time." "I have put Joan to bed poor girl is in such a state." "Ok sweetheart I will be five minutes." Jamie arrived at Liam's flat, it had one flight of stairs and at the bottom Liam kept his beloved mountain bike, so it was a bit of a squeeze for the first few steps. Millie had made some sandwiches for their dinner, she said Joan had gone to bed but wasn't hungry. "Jane is stopping at her friend's house tonight, so I am pleased you suggested we stopped the night Millie." "Poor Joan and Jane, hey Jamie?" "Are you ok?" a small tear rolled down Jamie's cheek. "I will miss my mate Millie" "I know" and she cuddled Jamie they ate the few sandwiches and Jamie said he wanted to finish Liam's diary. "Do you think that is a good idea tonight Jamie? You are already upset." "Yes I never knew this story, we only ever knew snippets and it's incredible. Years ago he said he was writing a diary and that he would leave it to me, I just thought he was joking. I wonder what made him finish it on the morning of his death Millie." "I don't know, it's a strange world we live in.

Millie was soon asleep and Jamie finished the diary amazed at the writing Jamie had produced. He turned the light off and was soon asleep himself. Millie woke up with a start. "What was that Jamie?" said

Millie, shaking him? "What?" "That noise is somebody trying to break in?" Flippin' heck Millie are you paranoid? It's 7.10 am in the morning" "Go and look" she begged. Jamie got up and put a light on in the living room, as he approached the stairs in anticipation that there might be somebody trying to break in, he shouted. "Millie quick call an ambulance, Joan is at the bottom of the stairs." Jamie shot down stairs, Joan breathed "He loved you Jamie, and then she slipped unconscious." The ambulance seemed to take an age, Jamie was frightened to move her. "Stand back Sir". There were two Paramedics, one was working on Joan, the other called the hospital "Have theatre ready we have a traumatized female approximately in her mid-forties we will be fifteen minutes."

Millie went in the ambulance and Jamie went off to find poor Jane. After trawling round a few pubs in town he found Jayne she didn't look like she was enjoying her night. Jamie had to tell what had happened. By now the poor girl was a wreck as they drove to the hospital. When they arrived Joan was already in the operating theatre. "What have they said Aunty Millie?" "Very little sweetheart, other than your Mum is in a serious condition." "Don't cry Jane, your mum is a fighter, she won't give up."

It was 8.30am when Joan was brought back from surgery heavily sedated. "Will she be ok nurse?" "I am sorry, I can't make a judgment, the brain surgeon Sir Leonard Grape will speak with you shortly." Three hours passed when eventually Sir Leonard Grape appeared and called them into his office, just off the side ward. Jamie couldn't look at him so much of the dairy was like recalling back to Jamie the 3.30am message. Was Sir Leonard Grape and Grape the man that Cabhan had killed connected? "I would suggest you spend time with Mrs Egan, I really don't think we can do anymore for her, but miracles do happen so we will give her twenty four hours and see what happens. If there is no sign of improvement then a decision will need to be taken. I am sorry. Nurse Aoi will be here for you should you need anything."

Jamie felt something really weird Nurse Aoi, wasn't she in the diary?

He couldn't say anything, but it was like Liam had been living his and Joan's demise. Between the three of them they took turns in sleeping Jane was holding her Mum's hand the whole time. It was exactly 7.10 am when the heart monitor flat lined, nurses came running from everywhere but Joan had slipped away.

Jane went to stop with Millie and Jamie, Jamie was obsessed with the diary he would read it over and over. The funeral date was set for Thursday 9th July. On the day of the funeral Liam's brother was there, all his friends and colleagues were in the little church that they had been married in.

Jamie knew he had to be strong for Millie and Jane, although deep inside he was hurting so much and even more so because he never fully believed Liam about the dreams and now having read the diary so many times, it was like that night all those years ago. Two troubled soul's

called Shona and Cabhan had found a
vehicle in Liam to explain what had
happened, then once they died so did
Liam and Joan. He tried to explain all that
to Millie but she just thought it was
dreams and the Ouija Board was just a
stupid game.

The little church was packed as the music
of Dolly Parton and Kenny Rogers sang
Islands in the stream, their favourite song.
The song ended and there was not a dry
eye in the congregation. "Ladies and
Gentlemen, could you all please stand for
our first hymn. Page three on the hymn
sheet, Morning Has Broken." Not many
people sang they were too busy wiping
tears away from their eyes. Jane clung to
Millie like a daughter to a mother.

The hymn finished and the vicar stood in
the pulpit. "Many years ago when I was a
young priest, I married a couple in this
very church they are the couple I am
sending on their journey to a new life
because as our lord said "Those of you
that believe in me shall not perish but
have everlasting life" "A very close friend

of the couple Mr Jamie Trench would like to say few words."

Jamie cleared his throat and climbed up to the pulpit. "Somebody once told me that men don't have many friends, only acquaintances. Well if that is true I must be honoured, as I have many friends but I had one very special friend, Liam Egan was his name. I met Liam through work when he came and worked alongside me all those years ago. Little did I know that over the years we would become like Siamese twins, we confided in each other there was nothing we could not tell each other. I was with Liam the night he met Joan this stunning lady chose him out of everybody in that club that night, it was like they were made for each other somehow." At this point, having read the diary, Liam had to try and hold it together his voice quivered and he cleared his throat again.

"Me and my wife adored Joan, and to be honest, when they got together, I was glad to get my wife back, because she was always cooking for Liam" and he smiled there was ripple of laughter in the congregation. "I wouldn't normally do this but I want to read this poem to my life mate and his beautiful wife."

"My heart's still active in sadness
and secret tears still flow
what it meant to lose you
No one can ever know.
But now I know you want us
to mourn you no more.

To remember all the happy times
Life still has much in store.
Since you'll never be forgotten
I pledge to you today
a hallowed place within my heart
is where you'll always stay".

"Egan's you are special and we lost you both that day. But I promise you this my friend, in our hearts you will always stay"

Jamie left the pulpit and could not help a small tear trickling down his cheek. The vicar stood up "If you could stand please for our second hymn, "For Those in Peril on the Sea"" Jamie was taking in all the coincidences and wondered if Liam had left a message.

The congregation seemed to have found their voices and once it was finished Jane went to the pulpit. "I can't believe how strong she is being Jamie," Millie whispered,

"My mum and dad. Let me tell you about my mum first. Mum looked like a super model all my friends at school used to comment and all the male teachers at Parent teacher evenings would try and flirt with her, much to my dad's annoyance. I would tease him telling him to look out, or she might run off with one of them. She never would have of course, she loved dad more than life itself, she often would say they had a special love from day one. People say I look like Mum I wish!! Mum called me Jane after the Rod Stewart song as this was a song she loved. She also gave me the name Shona which everyone comments on how unusual it is, but apparently it's a Caribbean name that also means Joan so she named me after herself. When she told me, I was probably about nine or ten and she asked me not to tell dad, I never did know why I just thought it was because he had been poorly." Jamie could feel upset in the pit of his tummy at this revelation.

"Let me tell you about my dad, he taught me to ride a bike, tie my shoe laces. He tried to show me how to make a poached egg, but I have to say he wasn't great at that. He protected me sometimes too much, but Mum said it was because he didn't know me in my early years and he was trying to make it up. You all today probably think I am being strong, but after Uncle Jamie's speech I realize how much I am like my wonderful parents, I love you both beyond words" and she touched both coffins and went back to the front pew,

It was almost three weeks before the will was read. Myself, Millie, Jane and Liam's brother Fergal were summoned to the offices of Drake and Baldwin, Joan and Liam's solicitors for the will reading.

"I am Archibald Drake and I have a joint will signed by Liam Egan and Joan Egan and witnessed by myself Archibald Drake on January 12th 2015." And he began to read.

"Being of sound mind and body this is the last will and testament of Liam Egan and Joan Egan of Poplar Flats Canary Wharf London England."

"To our daughter Jane Shona Egan, we leave all monies in our building society accounts with the Halifax, the Chelsea Building Society and our joint accounts at the Nat West and Barclays Banks. We also leave the flat at Canary Wharf and our apartment in Majorca. I Joan Egan, also leave all my personal effects to my daughter Jane Shona Egan."

"To my brother Fergal Egan, I leave my Panini football cards, because he always wanted my set." Fergal smiled. "I leave my wonderful brother my Audi Quatro and Joan's Mercedes SLK, simply for the fact he will be the only one careful enough on the roads I hope you don't mind. I also leave him my gym equipment and the book, a hundred ways to cook an egg, because he simply could not and that was possibly the only thing I was better at than my lovely brother Fergal."

Jane smiled and said "Uncle Fergal you must have been pretty poor at cooking eggs if Dad beat you." He smiled tears rolling down his cheeks and he hugged Jane,

"To my best friend Jamie, I leave you the job of scattering our ashes at Tree Cliff House, Claw Bay in County Mayo and you know why my friend. If you are hearing this then I thank you both for being the best friends we could ever have, please look after Jane for us"

Jamie could feel the sense of knowing, that Liam knew what was coming but only he had read the diary. Did he now share the story with Fergal and Jane or let the story die for fear of recreating things?

The will reading carried on, "Jamie, I also want you to have my Callaway golf clubs just so you can feel what it is like to win with them, seeing that I beat you almost every time we played mate. To the lovely adorable Millie, we leave you our Timeshare in the Caribbean and Joan's three Rolex watches. Finally, I want you Jamie, to have my watch. It need's attention but you always liked my Brietling."

"That is the full content of the last will and testament of Liam and Joan Egan. Thank you for your time today and the necessary actions will be taken for the things left you in the will, the personal effects mentioned I am sure Jane can give those to you all the other things will be made over to you in due course. Thank you for your time" and he stood up and showed us the door shaking our hands as we left.

On the way back to Liam's flat Jane was asking loads of questions about what her dad had said in the will. Jamie shrugged them off thinking that it was like a weird curse Liam had lived through since that night and that he seemed happier in Cabhan's world than his own.

Once back at the flat Jane and Fergal asked why they had chosen to have their ashes scattered at Claw Bay and what was the significance of Tree Cliff House. Jamie shrugged it off by saying they had a few days away a lot of years ago in Ireland doing the pubs round the West Coast and that they had dropped on this old run down house and Liam just fell in love with it. "Had Mum been there Uncle Jamie?" "I honestly don't know Jane." "Do you think we should scatter half over here and half in that place in Ireland?" Millie could see the concern on Jamie's face. "Jane why don't you scatter a handful of the ashes where you want and Uncle Jamie will spread the rest to the reading of the will." "I think that is a good idea Millie, what do you think Jane?" "Yeah I think so too Uncle Fergal. To be honest I think it would upset me if I went to Ireland. Would you mind if I just scattered a few of the ashes in the window box today Uncle Jamie, I feel I need closure." "Of course that's fine Jane."

Deep down Jamie didn't think it was a good idea but it was the best he could have hoped for and both he and Millie knew that.

Fergal then remarked that it was better if Jane scattered a handful today, as he was going with work to Dubai for a year and this would be his best chance, Jane took a handful of ashes out of the decorated green urn and said a few words scattering the ashes on her mother and fathers window boxes.

"Look if you are both ok, I think me and Jamie will make a move it's been a hard day. When Uncle Fergal goes back, you are more than welcome to come and stay with us Jane." "Thank you Aunty Millie, but I have to move on now, I intend to go to Hope University in Liverpool to study Caribbean Law." "You're Mum and dad would have been so proud, listen sweetheart I will call you in the week." Jamie and Millie left.

Once home Jamie went straight to his bedside cabinet and took out Liam's diary.

"Jamie, not tonight love." "There is something I am missing in this Millie, all these coincidences are just too much to believe that there is more to his dreams. Even Joan's name meant Shona, she found him remember? I told you about that night then she disappeared and magically re-appeared. In this diary Cabhan and Shona were parted." "Look Jamie we have lost two dear friends today and you are making out they were some kind of time travelers, just leave it. We can go to Claw Bay on Saturday then we leave this alone and we don't talk about the diary and we never ever tell Jane about this. I'm going to bed are you coming." "Will be with you in a while sweetheart." "Don't be long Jamie." "Ok."

Jamie made himself a coffee then he got a note pad and pen and started to read the diary again, noting anything that reflected present day. The amount of things similar was outstanding. The more he read, the more he felt his mate wanted him to investigate and possibly tell Jane the full story. How could a simple, silly game of Ouija have created all this, to the point of illness for Liam? What was the significance of Jamie waking at 3.30am and Joan dying at 3.30am? This was more than a coincidence. Jamie concluded that because Liam was· clearly Cabhan, in a previous life or maybe a parallel universe, and that Joan was Shona, even her name meant the same but in two different countries. Millie was shouting from the bedroom. "Liam come to bed, I can't sleep without you." Liam closed the diary quietly and put it on the TV cabinet.

The following morning all he could think about was looking at the diary. Millie was already up and dressed ready to drive to the ferry for Ireland to scatter the ashes. Liam dressed and his first thought was to get the diary and put in his carry-on luggage, before Millie could see or she might kick off and insist he left it at home. To his shock the diary wasn't where he left it by the TV. "Do you want a slice of toast with your coffee Jamie?" "Yes please." Millie must have moved it. He had no choice now he had to ask Millie. "Have you moved Liam's diary from the TV cabinet?" "Not that again Jamie, no I haven't, you are becoming obsessed with it." "I left it there, I know I did." "Come on Jamie or we will be late for the ferry." Jamie was frantically looking round the flat but finally decided he had no choice but to leave for the Pembroke to Rosslare ferry.

Millie had been driving about an hour. She always drove if they went out she said Jamie drove to fast. "Pass me a fruit pastel out of the glove compartment Jamie." Jamie opened the compartment and past Millie two pastels. "Thank you." "Have you got any other sweets in here? I don't like them." "Think there are some boiled sweets have a look." To Jamie's astonishment the diary was in the glove compartment. "Look what I found, you have hidden this you little Tinker." "No I haven't Jamie Trench. I have never even held the diary, you must have put it there last night." "I didn't Millie I know I didn't." "I know I should not say this but I will be glad when this is over and we can get back to some normality in our lives."

The rest of the journey was in abject silence as Jamie's head was buried in the diary. After a long drive they found a small pub that catered for Bed and Breakfast about 40 miles from Claw Bay. The pub was typical West Coast of Ireland; the ceilings were very low there was a cast-iron range in the corner with a fire roaring away. Six old locals sat around in various seats. The Landlord was quite a big man and he introduced himself Cain Fogarty. "How many nights will ye be staying with us?" "Just the one please, Mr Fogarty" "Sign there then and I'll show ye the room." They climbed a rickety staircase that creaked with every step they took. Fogarty showed them the room. It was clean but very old fashioned, with pictures of local views adorning the walls. "We get a lot of fishermen through the summer months. What is your business may I ask?" "We are heading for Claw Bay". Fogarty made a quick exit "Breakfast is from 6.30am to 9.00am and the bathroom is at the end of the corridor" and he left. "Blimey what is wrong with mine host Jamie?" "Not sure, but he didn't like us saying Claw Bay did he?"

Let's get cleaned up and go down for a couple of hours and have a drink and something to eat. The bar had filled up with a few more locals. It went very quiet and quite uncomfortable as they entered. Jamie nodded at a couple at the bar. They seemed relieved to have somebody to talk too.

"Hi I'm Jamie, this is my wife Millie". The couple was from Yorkshire. "Ted and Julie, pleased to meet you, are you on holiday?" "Only for a couple of day we are scattering the ashes of a couple of dear friends tomorrow at Claw Bay". Three old guys playing dominoes stopped playing drank their beer and left. "Did you say something wrong Jamie?" "It appears so Ted. What are you two up too?" "Well it's a long story, we are both retired and for many years I have been doing my family tree and I have a relative, who was the preacher, in a town not too far away called Timmid." Jamie almost spilt his beer. "You ok love?" "Yes, just went down the wrong hole. What is your family name then Ted?" "Ross and my many times removed granddad was the preacher in Timmid. So the plan is a few days in Timmid, then make our way round the coast, he is the last relative I have been able to track." They ordered another beer and meals and had quite a pleasant night, but Jamie could not wait to get back to the room and read the diary.

They wished Ted and Julie Ross a safe journey and left for their small bedroom. "No Jamie, you are not reading that damned diary!!" "Millie it's another coincidence, the preacher that married Cabhan and Shona, was called Ross. We are in the middle of nowhere and that couple introduce themselves and then go onto tell us they are going to Timmid, to trace a relative called Ross, who has the same name as the preacher who married Cabhan and Shona. Now you may think I am a fruit loop but are you not concerned with all these happenings." "I will tell you what I think. I think it is a collection of coincidences that you are trying to tie to Liam's story and that is because you don't want to let Liam go. I think once the ashes are scattered we should burn the diary."

"Millie, that is not going to happen, trust me." "I have never said anything before, but the Brietling Jamie left me, is stopped at 3.30 am." "Oh bloody hell Jamie, this is ridiculous get some sleep it will be an upsetting day tomorrow."

They were down for breakfast by 7.00 am so they could get off to Claw Bay, scatter the ashes and get back for the ferry.

The landlord seemed a bit more amiable. "Did you sleep well?" "Fine thank you" "We have a full Irish Breakfast available for you, would you like toast also." "No, I think looking at this breakfast it will keep us full until tomorrow, but thank you for the offer. Have Mr and Mrs Ross left yet?" "Yes they didn't have breakfast; they left at 6.00am this morning Sir." They finished the breakfast with no interruptions and while Jamie was putting the overnight bags in the car Millie paid the bill.

"I am sorry if you felt uncomfortable last night when the local lads walked out, but the English did some dreadful things in these parts and especially at Claw Bay. Many children and adults were murdered in cold blood. Nobody from these parts will go anywhere near Claw Bay, as you will see. They say you can hear the cries of the people murdered by the roundheads all those years ago Madam." Millie politely nodded and was really trying to push things like this out of her mind, she didn't want Jamie becoming obsessed like Liam had, because she knew deep down something was not right.

They set off for Claw Bay. "Seemed alright this morning that landlord." Millie nodded. "You ok Millie." "Yes just a bit upset, today is the day we finally say goodbye to them both." "Know what you mean, it's going to be tough." "Don't think I am daft, but I have written a little poem to read before we do the scattering". "Ah that is nice Jamie."

They left the car at the top of the lane leading down to Tree Cliff House. The path was even more overgrown than the last time when Liam and Jamie had visited. Jamie was holding Millie's hand

and the urn. As the house came into view Millie commented that she felt cold. "Here put my jacket on." "What about you?" "I will be fine." "I love you Jamie Trench," "I love you too Millie Trench."

They walked past the house towards the little chapel and around the side of the chapel to the cliff edge. "Ok, I'll put the urn down while I say a few words."

"Best friends are angels,
That God sent along.
They always stay beside you,
Whenever things go wrong.

We are glad that God blessed us,
With good friend's such as you.
Person's to be there,
Person's to get us through".

They both shed a tear as Liam opened the urn. It was a pleasant day with no wind. They both took a handful from the urn and threw it over the cliff before Jamie emptied the rest of the urn over the cliff. "Goodbye, my friends." They held each other and turned to walk away. Suddenly there was a loud curdling cry behind them Jamie spun round. "Did you hear that Millie?" They both rushed to the cliff edge all they could see were the waves crashing against the rocks and Claw Bay like a ghost town in the distance.

As they walked back Millie handed Jamie his coat back, "I feel ok now. We have to think what to do with the diary Jamie. You are correct, do we give it to Jane or not?" "I don't know what we have experienced over the past few years, but I know something it frightens the crap out of me Millie." "Me too and I don't want Jane having the same worries. I will put the diary in the loft when I get back I promise." As they walked past the derelict Tree Cliff House they both felt Liam's presence. Come on Jamie I want to go home, there are too many unexplained things in this place.

Once in the car Millie opened up to Jamie. "Look I do believe and understand what you are saying and I am sorry for having a go, I didn't mean that you don't want to let go of Liam, I know what he meant to you. I am just frightened that this diary thing could affect our lives like it did Liam's and there is also Jane to consider."

"But Millie, it's like Liam was purposely telling me to look into all this more deeply. Why would he give me a watch that stopped at 3.30am? All through the diary Liam doesn't understand why his dreams always end at 3.30am?" "I am guessing because that was when he died, Jamie". "Joan was Shona, he says she is her double, but a little taller. She also had the same mark made by the lead shot when they shot her." "How come the places he went to on his cruise, he remembered them as Cabhan?" "Millie, I am so glad you finally understand." "I think we have to wait and see if we have any dreams, if that doesn't happen, then maybe we should tell Jane the whole story Jamie."

"I think there is more still to come Millie and more will be revealed as time goes on. I agree Jamie the question is could this be the beginning of the journey or the end?"

Other books I have written are also on Amazon. The books are a series about a Peak District detective. This book is my first historical love story and maybe there will be more.

Printed in Germany
by Amazon Distribution
GmbH, Leipzig